DEATH
AT SEA

CHRISTOPHER BRYAN

Diamond Press

Death at Sea
Christopher Bryan

Printed in the Unites States of America
The Diamond Press
Sewanee, Tennessee

For more information about this book or the author, visit
www.christopherbryanonline.com

Edition ISBNs
Trade paperback: ISBN 978-0-9978496-3-9
e-book: ISBN 978-0-9978496-4-6

Library of Congress Cataloging-in-Publication data is available upon request.

First Edition 2019
Cover design by Kara Kosaka
Book interior by Short Run Press Ltd, Exeter
Diamond Press logo by Richard Posan for 2 Ps
Photograph of Christopher Bryan by Wendy Bryan

This book is a work of fiction. Names, characters, places, and incidents either are products of the author's imagination or are used fictitiously.

In memoriam
William Hoover Hethcock
March 19, 1932 – January 9, 2018

A faithful friend is a strong defence, and whoever
finds such a one has found a treasure.
Ecclesiasticus 6.14

DEATH AT SEA

ONE

Oak Cottage, 27 Durham Lane, Exeter.
10.45 pm Monday, 3rd September 2018.

Detective Inspector Verity Jones, Exeter CID, zipped up her heavy blue raincoat and pulled the hood over her head.

"You'll need to put your rain stuff on." Joseph's voice floated down from the bedroom where he was checking on their toddler Samuel. "It's raining cats and dogs! And blowing a gale!"

She gave a faint smile. "I know. I'm on it."

Hoover the dog, about to be taken for her final walk of the day, bounced about the hall excitedly.

"I doubt you'll be so excited when we get out there," Verity said, bending to fasten the lead.

She was right.

Once clear of the porch, Hoover's tail went down and she screwed up her eyes against driving rain. But she knew what was expected of her and plodded on manfully (or as one might say if there were such a word, dogfully) shoulders hunched, ears flapping in the wind. The sky flashed, and for the blink of an eye shining pavements and streaming gutters were drenched in cold light. Seconds passed, and there was a rumble of not very distant thunder.

Verity blew out her cheeks, blinked raindrops from her eyelashes and skirted round a particularly large puddle. The council really ought to do something about the pavement round here…

Ibant obscuri sola sub nocte per umbram…

They went on through shadow, hidden by lonely night…

Though at least Aeneas wasn't getting wet. Not so far as she could remember from her days of *Litterae humaniores*.

Finally they reached the end of the road where there was a patch of long grass with wildflowers and small, wet bushes tossing in the wind. Here, let off the lead, Hoover disappeared for several minutes and then reappeared, ears still flapping, eyes still screwed up, but with the satisfied look of one who despite all odds has done her duty.

She and Verity looked at each other with what was obviously much the same thought. Thank God, now we can go home.

Verity fixed the lead and they started back.

Another flash of lightning.

Another rumble of thunder, surely even nearer this time.

The rain was harder than ever.

Hello! What was this?

Adriana Martínez, who lived with her partner Jack Hooper in the house next door but one to Verity and Joseph, was standing coatless and bareheaded beside her garden gate, talking into her mobile. She was a small, pretty woman. Verity didn't know her well, but they'd drunk an occasional cup of tea together and she'd seen her and Jack a couple of times at church.

As she approached, over wind and driving rain and the banging of someone's loose gate she could hear Adriana's voice: anxious tones that became anxious words as she drew near.

"Jack, I'm really getting worried. Please phone me back when you get this. I just want to know you're all right…"

The woman lowered the phone and looked up.

"Hello," Verity said. "Is everything all right?"

That's a damned silly question, she told herself. Obviously everything isn't.

"It's Jack. He went out about eight, saying he was going to make sure the *Falcon* was secure before the storm hit."

Verity nodded. The *Falcon* was Jack Hooper's boat, which he clearly loved but also used to make a living.

"He didn't think he'd be gone for much more than an hour," Adriana said, "and here it is getting on for eleven and he still hasn't come home and I can't raise him. I've tried getting him on the landline and then on the mobile in case there was something wrong with the landline, and then I came out here to try because I thought maybe there was something wrong with the signal because of the storm and I wasn't getting through, but the phone says the signal's good and I don't know what to do."

Again Verity nodded.

"Where is the *Falcon*?"

"She's moored out at Topsham."

"Have you tried calling the harbour master?"

"Isn't it too soon?"

"It's what they're there for. And you can't stand out here all night. You'll catch your death. Come home with me. I'll call the harbour master. Let's see what they know."

Joseph fetched Adriana a cup of tea while Verity phoned the harbour master at Topsham.

"Yes," he said. "The *Falcon* went out some time ago. Let me check." There was a pause. "She left at 22.17."

"With the storm brewing?" she said.

"It does seem a bit crazy, heading out like that, but the vessel's in good order and of course he's a perfect right to sail whenever he likes."

"So you reckon all's well?"

"Let me see if we've got any radar fix on her."

There was another pause, this time several minutes. Then—

"Yes, given when he set out and the conditions, I'm pretty sure we have. Assuming it's the *Falcon*, he's sailed out about six and a half miles, and now it looks as though he's riding it out. It's rough weather, but he's a competent sailor. The *Falcon*'s got all the right equipment so he could let us know if he was in any trouble. He's out of the main shipping lanes, so he's no hazard to anyone. I don't know why he isn't answering any calls, and I don't know why he didn't tell his partner he was going out. But it doesn't look from here that there's anything wrong."

He hesitated a moment.

"Look," he said, "the coastguard's a bit overwhelmed at the moment, but if he's still there at first light we'll have someone go out and check on him."

Verity replaced the phone and looked at Adriana and Joseph.

"He says Jack went out at just before twenty past ten and looks from the radar to be okay, just riding out the storm. But they will go out and check on him at first light."

"Thank you so much," Adriana said, looking somewhat happier. "Though I still don't understand. Going out like that—it's not like him."

Verity gave what she hoped was a reassuring smile.

But she too was puzzled. Why *would* he go out like that?

"Let's have another cup of tea," she said.

Two

Magdalen Road, Exeter. The following morning.

Above the squish of tyres on wet tarmac Detective Superintendent Cecilia Anna Maria Cavaliere, Exeter CID, could
hear birds chirping from trees near the almshouses in Magdalen
Road. The air coming at her through the open car window was
cool and fresh.

She slowed as they passed something called "Leela", where off-
white plaster proclaimed there were "ethical gifts and clothes" to
be had. How very odd. Were clothes not ethical? Or were they only
not ethical if given as gifts? Next was Lloyd's Pharmacy, Victorian
redbrick bonding uneasily with a thoroughly twenty first century
automatic door. Still, no doubt their more fragile clients were glad
of the door.

The car splashed though a large puddle—the road was uneven
here and last night's storm had left swathes of water—and came to
a stop at the lights. On her left now, more Victorian red brick: the
Mount Radford pub, in its own way rather elegant, lit chandeliers
and twinkling brass shining through plate glass windows. Someone in a white apron was cleaning the brass.

People with early morning hurry on their faces streamed across the road in front of her. Several appeared to be talking to themselves. When she was a little girl she'd have thought they must be mad. Now she spotted the little white plugs in their ears and guessed they were just on the phone. Talking of which—

The mobile on her dashboard was flashing. It was the Heavitree Police Station.

She touched the screen.

"Cavaliere here," she said.

"It's Verity! Sorry to call you on your late morning, but we may have a situation."

It was a Tuesday, what everyone referred to as Cecilia's "late morning"—the day of the week when instead of her being at the station by seven she and Michael—the Reverend Michael Aarons, Rector of St Mary's—were able to have breakfast with the children and act like normal people.

So why did "situations" always seem to arise on her "late morning"?

"Sod's Law!" Michael whispered, sitting next to her and evidently guessing her unspoken question.

She chuckled.

"We're just taking Rachel to school and then Michael to the cathedral," she said. "All right if I call you back after? Should be ten minutes at most."

"Perfect," Verity said.

The phone went dead. The lights changed.

Right turn into St Leonard's Road: prosperous nineteenth century residential houses. Left onto Wonford: more of the same, with a certain quirky untidiness—black and green council rubbish bins, overgrown hedges and a general air of genteel muddle. And then right onto Matford Road and on towards the grounds of County Hall.

They were approaching the school.

There was the usual crowd of cars disgorging children.

Eight-year-old Rachel in the back seat began gathering her things together.

"Oh, by the way," she said. "I won't be out until four this afternoon."

"Why's that?" Cecilia asked.

"I'm in detention."

Cecilia raised an eyebrow as she brought the car to a halt behind a white Toyota Prius.

"So why are you in detention?" she asked, looking at her daughter through the rear view mirror.

"Mr Bolger was doing class registers and asked me when my birthday was."

"So?"

"I told him the twenty second of June."

"And?"

"He said, 'What year?'"

"So?"

"So I said, 'Every year.'"

Michael guffawed, hastily and unconvincingly changing it to a cough.

Cecilia rolled her eyes, and Rachel flashed him a brilliant smile.

"So what happened next?" Cecilia said.

"Mr Bolger said, 'Stop trying to be funny!' and put me in detention."

"And were you trying to be funny?"

There was a very slight pause.

"Yes."

Cecilia turned round to gaze directly at her longhaired, leggy and utterly self-confident daughter.

"Well," she said after a moment, "judging by papa's reaction you succeeded. Four o'clock it is, then."

For a few seconds they watched as the child scampered off happily to join her friends.

"You'd better call Verity," Michael said.

"You're all right for time?"

"I've got lots of time. Go for it!"

Verity filled her in briefly with the events of the previous evening, and then said, "So the coastguard sent someone out at first light to check on him. The boat's all right but I'm afraid Jack Hooper is dead."

"Oh dear God!" Michael said softly and made the sign of the cross.

"It looks," Verity continued, "like an accident in the storm— apparently the boom came across suddenly and hit him on the head. But for some reason the coastguard isn't happy about it. Wants us to take a look. As it's a possibly suspicious death, I thought you'd want to know."

"I certainly do."

"I told them to treat the vessel as a potential crime scene until we get there. And I called the marine section and they're fixing someone to collect us at Topsham quay and take us out. I'm waiting for them to call me back."

"I take it you've told Jack Hooper's partner—Adriana?"

"She's in a bit of a state, which is understandable. But it helps that we've known each other a while and Joseph was great with her. And then Brenda Cosgrove—you know her, don't you, the PC from uniform?—she's there now. She's a warm sort of person. I told her to take as long as it needed."

Cecilia did indeed know Brenda Cosgrove. She was just the right person.

"Excellent. As usual you seem to have thought of everything. All right then—expect me at the station in about fifteen minutes, depending on the traffic."

So much for her late morning!

THREE

Exeter. About twenty minutes later.

Cecilia took Michael to the Cathedral, where he was to spend most of the day at a meeting on diocesan and cathedral finances, which were rocky. (Whenever was *that* news?—their friend John, sometime Curator of Antiquities in the city's Royal Albert Museum, had recently shown them a medieval document in which the dean and chapter were complaining to the city about cathedral's lack of decent revenues *in middle of the fifteenth century!*)

Cecilia shook her head at this thought, and having dropped her husband in South Street, where it was easy for him to walk through the Close to the Deanery, drove on via Western Way and the Paris Street Roundabout to Heavitree Police Station.

The previous night's storm had served, among other things, to show how much the station car park needed resurfacing. The sun was shining and things were beginning to dry out, but still there were pools of water everywhere. As she walked towards the main building Cecilia had to pick her way between them, enjoying as she did so the bright, clear light and the plash and squish of tyres as other vehicles entered the park. Sparrows chirped, hopping here and there among small bits of debris to see if there were anything in it for them, and a there was a clean, after-the-storm air over all.

She entered the station and realized how glad she was to be there. Back in January everyone at Heavitree had thought they were on the verge of major changes. Chief Superintendent Glyn Davies' long-time friend and one-time army colleague Ian Salmon—Commander Salmon of the National Crime Agency—had died. The powers-that-be had determined that Glyn Davies would be his replacement in London. The Chief Constable of Devon and Cornwall then nominated Cecilia to be Chief Superintendent at Heavitree in his place.

Cecilia had faced this prospect with mixed feelings. She enjoyed being a detective and working with her team, and she didn't at all look forward to the politicking and committees with which the chief superintendent was inevitably involved. But still, someone had to replace him and those whose judgment she respected seemed to think she was the one. So after long conversations with Michael and considerable wrestling with herself, she'd accepted.

But then, without any warning, someone even greater among the powers-that-be—someone at HM Treasury—had decreed that "for reasons of economy" Commander Salmon would not be replaced *at all*.

It looked like one more example of, "they keep on wanting us to do more and more with less and less"—a constant refrain these days, leading some wit at the station to suggest "they'll be setting the bloody thing to music next."

A more biblically educated generation, Michael observed, might have talked about having to make bricks without straw.

Whatever one's choice of allusion or metaphor, one thing was clear: everyone at Heavitree would stay where they were.

The odd thing was that Cecilia, having accepted the changes reluctantly, found herself irritated, even resentful, when they fell through. She hadn't wanted the job and then she was angry because she wouldn't get it! And since being angry about not getting something she didn't want was manifestly absurd, she was also angry with herself for being angry!

It had taken her a surprising length of time to get over this ridiculous state of mind, but her sense of pleasure as she looked round at the familiar morning bustle told her that indeed she *had* got over it. Even the ghastly but ubiquitous blue and cream paint today seemed somehow friendly. She was glad to be where she was.

"Good morning, ma'am."

DC Headley Jarman greeted her as she approached the Serious Crimes office.

"Should I take my jacket off?"

He grinned. "Probably not."

Verity Jones, who was not only Cecilia's long time friend but also her number two in "Serious Crimes", appeared in the doorway.

"So what's the latest?"

"The marine section just called. There'll be someone waiting at Topsham quay to take us out at 8.45."

Cecilia glanced at the clock on the wall, and then looked at Headley Jarman.

"You were right," she said. "I didn't need to take my jacket off!"

FOUR

Morning traffic was heavy on the Topsham Road—as, indeed, it always seemed to be these days—and by the time Cecilia and Verity arrived at the harbour one of the marine section's offshore rigid hulled inflatables was already moored by the quay, waiting to go. The young officers crewing the vessel introduced themselves: PCs Meg Hopkins and Ruth Dunstan.

"Are you ready for a sail, ma'am?"

PC Hopkins at the helm pointed behind her.

"There are lifejackets you can use."

Cecilia smiled inwardly, recognizing "can" as polite euphemism for "must, since it's regulations".

They wasted no time casting off, and were soon moving through the Exe Estuary, downriver past wide sand flats on their right, with thousands of birds, many of whose names Verity knew.

"There's an avocet!" she said, and then, "Those are dunlins! They like to fly in flocks to confuse the predators. But surely this is very early? I thought they didn't come 'til January."

"Everything's weird this year," PC Dunstan said. She nodded toward a small dark silhouette that was drifting between the flock and the sun. "But there's your predator. All England to a pinch of snuff he's a peregrine falcon, that one, and he's planning his dinner!"

On their left they were now passing Lympstone village, dominated from the river by the long grey-brick buildings of the Royal Marines' Commando Training Centre.

"Lots of dishy men leaping about," PC Dunstan said, and indeed they could see some of the marines training.

"And a few dishy women," said PC Hopkins.

After Lympstone came Cockwood (pronounced "Cockoude" by the properly informed), where Cecilia had enjoyed many a sea-food meal with Michael at the Anchor pub.

And so finally they put out into Lyme Bay and the English Channel, where the inflatable began to rock as the crew put on speed. They were now in open waters, which after last night's storm were still quite choppy enough to remind them that though human chauvinism might call this a channel, it was a link between two oceans and not to be trifled with.

The Jurassic coastline fell astern, showing sharp and sunlit against a now brilliant sky. The regular *"Plash! Plash!"* of waves slapping against the inflatable's bow stirred Cecilia's heart, and she realized somewhat guiltily that despite the mournful purpose of their journey she was actually enjoying it.

The *Falcon*, a pretty vessel flying the red ensign, looked trim and tidy as they approached, with its sails reefed and a coastguard vessel beside it, blue ensign fluttering in the breeze.

"Is that the kind of boat you could take right out to sea?" Cecilia asked the maritime officers.

"Blue water? Oh yes, ma'am. That's a Valiant 42—cutter-rigged sloop. Tankage is a bit light for anything very long, but she's tough and she's nimble."

Cecilia nodded.

She could see the uniformed figures of two coastguards watching as the police vessel came up, and she recognized their insignia: a Maritime Operations Officer and a trainee.

Minutes later they were on board. The senior of the two coastguards introduced himself and his colleague: Maritime Operations Officer Jack Smith and Trainee Maritime Operations Officer George Jarman.

"Are you related to Headley Jarman who's with Exeter CID?" Cecilia asked.

"He's my cousin, ma'am," the trainee replied.

"So law enforcement runs in the family, then."

"Yes, ma'am."

She smiled. "It does in mine, too." There had been generations of Carabiniere in the Cavaliere family.

Together they surveyed the crumpled body of Jack Hooper, his head battered and bloodied, lying just below the boom on a much creased tarpaulin, amid pools of water between the creases.

"And you've touched nothing?" Cecilia said. "Beyond making sure he was dead?"

"Absolutely not, ma'am," Officer Smith said. "That and we checked the rest of the vessel to make sure there was no one else on board—which there isn't."

"Good. And I gather you're not happy about this being an accident?"

"I'm not," the coastguard said. "I understand how accidents like this can happen. He was alone, it was dark, and the weather was foul. Anyone could get caught out in that situation. But I knew Jack Hooper a bit. And what I *can't* understand is why he would get himself into a situation like this in the first place. What possible reason could he have had to cast off from a secure mooring and take his boat out to sea in a thunderstorm in the middle of the night? It just doesn't fit with the man I knew."

Verity was nodding.

"I had the same thought when I talked with the harbour master last night," she said.

"So what's your thought now, DI Jones?" Cecilia said.

Verity gazed quizzically at the body for several minutes. She walked round it, looking at it from several angles.

"I suppose there were no breaks in the rain last night?" she said. "Out here, I mean?"

He shook his head. "Not a chance. It never stopped pouring from—oh, ten o'clockish, I'd say, until about six this morning."

Verity nodded, and stood still.

"Then this can't have been an accident during last night's storm," she said. "The state of the blood makes it impossible."

Cecilia gave a rueful little smile. "I agree."

"The blood?" the coastguard said.

"As you've just pointed out, it was pouring with rain from ten 'til six," Cecilia said. "Everything is soaked, including the body. If the boom had knocked him down during the storm, the rain would have washed the blood away. As it is," she pointed, "there's quite a lot of it round the wound and it's congealed. So it looks as though he actually died somewhere *out* of the rain, where the body stayed long enough for the blood to dry. Then he was brought out here and dumped on the deck under the boom to make it *look* like an accident."

She paused.

"Which sounds very like murder," she added, stating the obvious.

The coastguard looked at his younger colleague who smiled and shook his head. "Why on earth didn't we see that?"

"Don't worry," Cecilia said. "It's what they pay us for."

"And what we're actually saying," Verity said, "is we think you were right to be suspicious. What's more, if in fact he was murdered, that probably answers your other question. Presumably it wasn't Jack Hooper at all but his killer who decided to go to sea in a storm. And I guess the killer might think the storm was a real piece of luck, since it offered the perfect setting for a fake accident."

"But then," the coastguard said after a moment, "the problem with all that is there's no one else on board. If Jack Hooper was murdered and then brought out here by who-ever-did-it, how the hell did whoever-did-it then get away?"

Cecilia looked at Verity, who raised her eyes to the heavens and shook her head.

"That," Cecilia said, turning her gaze back to the coastguard, "is a very good question."

She frowned. "No-evidence-of-presence" is not necessarily "evidence-of-absence", but still that did not answer the coastguard's question.

"What about the killer having his own boat in tow and leaving in that? Or another vessel coming and taking the killer off?" she said. "Or would that have been impossible during the storm?"

The coastguard shook his head. "Difficult but not impossible—the RNLI do it all the time. But it didn't happen. I've already checked the record on the *Falcon*'s radar. Of course he had it on last night during the storm and it was still on. Look, you can see for yourselves."

They followed him and peered together at the small screen.

"There," he said, "is the *Falcon*. As you can see, it's alone for the whole night. And here," he pointed to a moving blip on the screen, "is the first vessel to come out to it—that's us, earlier this morning. And there's the second. You. Just now."

They straightened up and looked at each other.

"Might they have swum?" Verity said.

The coastguard gave a sharp intake of breath and shook his head. "It was blowing a gale, the sea was violent, it was pitch dark and we're nearly seven miles out. I'm not saying it's absolutely impossible, but..." He shrugged.

"Dam' nearly impossible," Verity said. "Point taken."

"Let's say if they *did* swim, then you are looking for an amazing swimmer," he said.

"Or perhaps you're looking for a drowned corpse," the trainee pointed out. "Maybe the killer just *tried* to swim."

There was a pause while they considered this suggestion.

"Well," Cecilia said, "this is certainly a puzzle. Despite that, given what we've got, I'm treating this as a suspicious death. I want the *Falcon* towed back to the quay and secured as a crime scene, and then I'll be wanting an MIT to go over it."

"MIT?"

"Murder Investigation Team. Verity, will you organize that?"

Verity nodded. "I'm on it, ma'am."

FIVE

The Quay at Topsham. Later that morning.

V erity was indeed "on it", as were HM Coastguards. They had the *Falcon* to Topsham Quay and moored by mid-morning. The vessel was at once secured as a crime scene, and within the hour a Murder Investigation Team—what Verity's husband Joseph liked to refer to as "Tom Foss and his minions"—arrived from Exeter in their tech vans and moved in, looking, as they always did, oddly like spacemen. All this to the evident delight and fascination of customers sitting at The Lighter Inn across from the quay, who had an excellent view of the goings on as they drank their ale and ate early lunches in the pub yard. Even clientele of the world famous Topsham Quay Antiques Centre were seen to pause and gaze at the scene as they entered and left the building, hoping perhaps (even against hope) to see some manacled felon led forth from the *Falcon* to justice.

Among those who sat and drank their ale was a small, balding man in a dark suit. He was well aware that he looked as if he were taking time off from the office, which indeed he was—*his* office. His secretary had a sign on her desk, which he pretended not to notice: "Would you like to talk to the man in charge or the woman who knows what's going on?" Of course she had no idea what was going on, which was just as well for her. But he was very sure she had one thing right. He *was* the man in charge.

After a while he took a sip from his tankard. He replaced it on the table, careful to centre it precisely on the circular beer mat next to his mobile phone. He dried his lips on a napkin, which he refolded and laid on the other side of the tankard and at right angles to it.

The blue and white "police-line-do-not-cross" tapes, the uniformed officer who stood behind them with folded arms, the arrival and prompt admission of what he'd immediately recognized as a Murder Investigation Team, all told him that Jack Hooper was dead. That was the good news. The bad news was that Hooper's demise was supposed to look like an accident. And the scene before him showed clearly that for some reason they'd been rumbled. The local plods weren't buying it.

The mobile phone vibrated. He picked it up, listened for a few seconds and then said, "Well never mind all that. What about what I paid you for?"

"Already handled. Hooper is history. Why do you ask?"

"Because you were supposed to make it look like an accident. And not to put too fine a point on it, the reason why Hooper's yacht is now full of people crashing around all over it is that you've gone and made a balls-up. That's why."

Six

Whatever the jokes at his expense, Tom Foss knew his business and was not one to waste time. He was able to phone Cecilia at Heavitree with a preliminary report on Jack Hooper's death by late afternoon.

"He died of severe trauma resulting from a blow to the head. The time of death between 9.30 and 10.30 last night."

"So very possibly he died before the *Falcon* left the harbour at 10.17? Which would mean someone else took the boat out, as we guessed."

"Very possibly, even probably."

"Good. Anything else?"

"Two things. First, whatever caused the trauma that killed your man, I'm sure it wasn't the *Falcon*'s boom. You were quite right to notice the blood on him had congealed—which wouldn't have happened if he'd died in all that heavy rain. What you couldn't know, but we've found, is blood in the main cabin. Someone's tried to clean it up, but there's quite enough left for us to find—on the carpet and on the steps up to the deck, and there's been blood spatter on the cabin ceiling. As I'm sure you know, it's very hard to remove bloodstains completely. When we have the DNA results, I'll be very surprised if they and the victim's blood don't give us match. If they do, then the obvious conclusion is he was killed in the cabin and then the corpse was moved to the deck so as to fake an accident. Which I think is what you surmised."

Cecilia nodded. "Excellent, Tom. And the other thing?"

"It looks as though the victim put up a fight before the blow that killed him. There's some bruising on his knuckles, which suggests to me he got in a couple of decent blows of his own, and then I guess whoever it was got lucky with the cudgel—or whatever it was. I saw no sign of the murder weapon, incidentally."

Cecilia nodded.

"Anyway," he continued, "we're ready to release the body to the coroner's office so they can schedule the inquest. The paramedics are to be here at four to collect it. And we should be back on dry land by four-thirty. I shan't be sorry, frankly."

"Some special reason?"

"I've never worked on a small boat before. That cabin *creaks* at times for absolutely no reason! I find it quite unnerving."

Cecilia laughed. The thought of Tom Foss—who to her knowledge had investigated some pretty gruesome murders in his time—being unnerved by a creak was quite funny.

"Never mind," he added. "It's nothing a dram or so of Glenmorangie at home this evening won't put right."

She nodded. She was a wine-and-occasional-beer girl herself, and knew little about highland single malts. But she'd learnt enough over her years of working with Tom Foss to recognize the names of a few of them and to know he was something of an aficionado.

"I take it," he said, "you still want the *Falcon* secured as a crime scene?"

"Indeed I do," she said. "Now more than ever. Verity's arranged all that with local uniform."

"By the way," he added, "BBC Southwest and the ITV lot

turned up at about two. Of course we didn't talk to them. Strictly no comment."

"That's all right. Glyn Davies and I talked to them and the press. They have their pretty pictures and we seem to have satisfied them for the moment as far as information is concerned. Glyn Davies even had a discreet word with the locals after the conference, and I think he's persuaded them to lay off the victim's partner at least for today. Pointed out that it would give them a new angle for a follow-up tomorrow. And then added that we'd been very forthcoming and co-operative with them so far, and we might be some more. So it'd be in their interest to keep us sweet. He's rather good at that, you know, chatting up the media. I think the woman from BBC Southwest fancies him. It's all that Welsh charm."

Tom Foss chuckled. "Carrot and stick! Yes, he is good with them. And I doubt our little story will make it nationally."

No, Cecilia thought, I doubt it will. We're far too full of the British government not having a clue what it's doing about Brexit, with the latest antics of the US president as occasional comic relief.

But all she said was, "No, I don't imagine it will."

The call finished, she sat back in her chair and looked at her team—Verity, the two DCs Headley Jarman and Tom Wilkins, and of course Joseph, the only civilian in the team, who in addition to being a Bahamian and Verity's husband was also their computer expert—indeed, genius, as she had often found—and could research anything.

"Well," she said, "you heard all that"—she'd kept the call on speakerphone—"so you know as much as I do. Verity—you've got Topsham uniform keeping an eye on the *Falcon* tonight?"

"Covered, ma'am. And I've arranged for some uniformed constables to go round the harbour door-to-door and boat-to-boat, in case anyone's noticed anything. We could do with a few witnesses."

"We certainly could."

"And Joseph's checking for any CCTV footage that may tell us anything."

Joseph nodded. "I'm on it."

"Good." Cecilia looked at the two Detective Constables. "Tom, Headley, I want you two to head out to Topsham first thing tomorrow morning and comb the *Falcon* from top to bottom—stem to stern, whatever. Photographs, documents, letters, anything that might give us a clue as to who might have murdered Jack Hooper, why anyone would want to, and how on earth they managed to scarper after doing it. You know what to do."

The two young detectives nodded.

"Right."

"We'll be there, ma'am."

She looked again at Joseph.

"Joseph, I want background. Starting with Jack Hooper himself and Adriana Martínez. Finances, jobs, who they know, what they know, whatever. You know the drill. I presume as we go forward there'll be others to check on, but those two to start with."

Joseph nodded. "On it, ma'am."

"Verity, I'll come over to you tomorrow morning first thing, and let's go and interview Adriana Martínez. Perhaps *she* knows who might want to murder her partner. Obviously she can't have killed him herself, since she's got the perfect alibi."

Verity grinned. "Me!"

"Exactly! Though she might have got someone else to do it while she played the worried partner. You never know."

"Or," Verity said, "if he had a secret life that got him killed, she wouldn't be the first woman who hadn't a clue what her partner was up to while he was out of the house."

Cecilia nodded. "Indeed she wouldn't." There was a pause. "So—anything else? Am I missing something?"

"There may be papers in their house. Something informative," Verity said.

"Right. Will you get someone to check that?"

"We can take a look ourselves when we go to see her tomorrow," Verity said.

Cecilia nodded. Of course they could.

"If she's involved she'll have had plenty of opportunity by then to clear away anything incriminating," Headley pointed out.

"If she's involved, I dare say she'll have done that already," Cecilia said. "But if she isn't, there may still be a desk that he used or something like that with something useful in it."

There was a pause.

"Anything else?"

This time there were blank looks and shaking heads.

"Right. We've all got tasks for the first part of tomorrow. Let's say we meet together here at three, put the results together, and see where we are then."

Everyone nodded.

She glanced at the clock. "And since I don't see what else we can do tonight, I suggest we all go home now and try to live our lives. We can come back at it with fresh minds tomorrow."

This, clearly, was a suggestion that met with general approval.

SEVEN

The Quay, Topsham, by the Falcon. That night, 11.15 pm.

No one could reasonably have claimed that the Quay at Topsham was badly lit, but still there were areas of shadow. Two young men, one rather tall, one quite short, appeared suddenly out of one of them, looming from the darkness as if from nowhere. They were weaving their way towards the *Falcon*'s gangplank.

PC Sam Devlin, who with his colleague PC Annwn Merchant was on duty until midnight, stepped forward quickly and barred their way.

You could smell the beer a mile off.

"I'm afraid this is off limits, sir. As you can see—it's a police crime scene."

"We are aware of that fact, officer," said the smaller of the two, speaking slowly and with alcoholic dignity, "and we are *endeavouring* to visit it. We are here to offer our services. We will assist you in your investigation."

Sam looked at Annwn, who put on her most engaging smile.

"And just exactly how would you be proposing to do that, sir?" she said.

The taller of the two stepped forward, swaying only very

slightly. "We are from the university," he said. "We have trained minds. And a trained mind can always focus on the task at hand and… and…" He trailed away.

"Bring lucid insights to bear on it," his small companion interjected.

"Tha's right," said the other.

"I see, sir," she said politely. "Well, of course, that's very good of you. But you'll need authorization."

She looked at her colleague.

"Perhaps they could be made into special constables," he offered.

"There you are!" she said, "You could become special constables! But you'd need to ask about that at the station. In Heavitree."

"Then to Heavitree we shall go!"

"Sir," she said hastily, "you aren't thinking of *driving* to Heavitree, are you? *Not now*, I mean?"

"Of course not officer. If you knew how drunk I am, you would not make such an improper suggestion."

"Probably not, sir," Annwn said.

Sam just stopped himself from laughing.

"My mother is Mrs Cornellissen," the small one continued loftily. "Mrs Letitia Cornellissen of Ambrose house—just around the corner. We shall sleep there to night and arrange to become special constables tomorrow."

"Good idea, sir."

"Officers and guardians of the law, we bid you good night."

"Good night, sir."

The two figures wove their way off into the gloom.

"Were they for real?" Sam said, gazing after them.

"Oh, I dare say they were real enough. Pissed as newts, but real."

"That name he said sounded foreign. Cornell—what was it?"

"Cornellissen," she said. "It's Dutch. There are quite a few

Dutch in Topsham. Have been since the sixteenth century. There was a lot of trade with Amsterdam. Even some of the architecture's Dutch."

"They didn't *sound* foreign. Posh, but not foreign."

She shook her head. "When I say Dutch, I mean it's their ancestors were Dutch. Now they're just typical upper-class English twits. They'll probably end up running daddy's business."

Sam shook his head. "Jeez, no wonder the country's falling apart."

An hour or so had passed, and it was getting on for one a.m., when they were to be relieved.

There was a sudden bang from the deck of the *Falcon*.

The two looked round, then at each other.

"You watch here," Sam said, "I'll yell if I need backup!"

"Go for it!"

He ran up the gangplank and round to the far side of the deck.

Certainly no one had passed them, but perhaps someone had rowed out quietly to the *Falcon* and was trying to board it from the seaward side?

He rounded to the far side of the cabin, his pulses pounding with excitement, and stopped.

It was deserted.

He looked out across the harbour.

The water was calm and untroubled.

He walked up and down. He shone his powerful LED torch into nooks and crannies, around the mainmast, folded tarpaulins, lifebuoys, up and down, forward and aft. There was no one.

Annwn's voice came up from the quay. "Are you all right, Sam?"

"I'm fine," he shouted back

"What's going on?"

"I'm trying to find out."

Finally he returned to the quay.

"Nothing!" he said, switching off the torch. "False alarm. Maybe it was a gull or something landing on the deck. They're bloody big birds. It could have banged into a tarpaulin or the mast or something. I suppose that would have made a row."

Did gulls fly around at night? Were they that clumsy? He had no idea.

But Annwn was nodding.

"All right, then. I suppose it could be that." She paused. "Well I'm sure no one got past us."

"So am I—but I did think for a minute maybe someone could have rowed across the harbour and boarded from the seaward side. Anyway, they didn't. There's no one there."

A police Panda car pulled onto the quay.

"And here's our relief," he said. "I don't know about you but I'm about ready for a break."

EIGHT

Oak Cottage. The following morning: Thursday, 6th September.

Cecilia was already tired when she arrived at Verity and Joseph's neat little house and rang the bell. Michael, having spent most of the previous day in a diocesan meeting, had then had to attend a parish meeting in the evening from which he had come home late and exhausted. But then he hadn't slept well and had snored when he did, so she hadn't slept well either. As a result they'd both overslept, woken irritated with themselves and each other, and then had to rush round getting Rachel and Rosina ready for the day, walking dogs and feeding everyone without time even to make coffee for themselves.

Fortunately Verity and Joseph seemed to be starting the morning in rather better order. Hoover greeted her with a friendly woof and wagging tail, and Joseph offered her a cup of tea, which she gladly accepted. Feeling somewhat revived by this, she eventually set off with Verity to see if Adriana Martínez was at home.

She was. She looked tired and a little red-eyed but was perfectly calm and appeared willing enough to talk with them about what had happened and about her relationship with Jack Hooper. They were shown into a modest but pleasantly furnished sitting room, where they were offered tea, which they accepted. Cecilia didn't really need a second cup, but Michael always emphasized how important it was to accept people's hospitality if you wanted to establish a rapport with them, and over the years she'd come to the conclusion that he was right. Cup of tea in hand, she settled herself to listen. She'd also long ago discovered for herself that it generally paid to start by letting people tell you whatever they wanted to tell you in their own way. Questions, crosschecking and requests for explanation—all those could come later.

Adriana Martínez said that she and Jack had been living together now for about six years, although they'd first met some years before that at a charity thing for Barnardo's. He'd been orphaned when he was very little and Barnardo's had helped him grow up and he was making a short speech about it. And she'd been one of the undergraduates from the university doing good works and helping organize the evening. He'd asked her out and they'd had a couple of dates together. But then they'd lost touch and only linked up again when he came to settle in Devon after a few years. He now made his living by using his boat: exploring the coast, taking people over to France, groups that wanted to fish, groups who wanted to look at the Jurassic coast, that sort of thing. They were all the kind of people who liked to hire him and the *Falcon*.

What about her? What did she do?

She was a librarian, and worked in the university library.

Sometimes she'd gone out with Jack on his hires if she was free and it was a small party and there was room. She'd always thought he was a wonderful sailor and very careful about safety. That was why she could hardly believe it when the harbour man said he'd taken the *Falcon* out with a storm brewing. That just wasn't the sort of thing he'd do.

Cecilia nodded.

They came to the question that always had to be asked.

"Can you think of anyone who might have wanted to kill Jack?" she said.

Adriana Martínez sighed and shook her head.

"Honestly," she said after a moment, "I can't. I mean, of course I've been thinking about that ever since Verity told me what's happened. Certainly Jack got across people at times—he got across me sometimes! He was noisy and bouncy and he liked silly little—"

She stopped for moment and caught her breath. Cecilia and Verity waited quietly.

"He liked his silly little jokes," she said finally, "and some people found that annoying. But as for killing him! That's ridiculous. I can't understand how anyone can possibly have thought of him in that way. He was kind. He'd had a bit of a rough life when he was young. But he was kind. He could be so gentle. I don't know how I'm going to go on without him."

Her mouth quivered and there was a pause.

"He'd started coming to church with me a bit," she said after a minute.

Verity nodded. "I know. We'd seen you. I'm sorry I never got to speak with you at church."

"Oh that's all right. And your Joseph did once or twice. Quite a long chat Jack had with him one time. But we tended mostly to slip away after the service. Jack was a bit shy about—church people. But Father Michael was always nice."

Cecilia bit her lip. Dear God, the woman and her partner had been attending Michael's church and she'd never even noticed!

"Jack liked Father Michael," Adriana Martínez continued. "He's coming round a bit later. He phoned yesterday and said how he'd heard about Jack and how sorry he was and could he come round this morning so I said yes."

Cecilia nodded.

"You said Jack had a bit of a rough life when he was young,"

Verity said. "Do you know anything about that? Might he have had any enemies from that part of his life?"

"He didn't talk about it much. He was ten years older than me—some people said that wasn't good, but we didn't care."

Cecilia swallowed a smile. Her father was fourteen years older than her mother, and Michael was eight years older than she was.

"Jack never really knew his parents," Adriana said. "They'd been killed in a car crash when he was five. But then he'd been helped a lot and fostered by Barnardo's. He swore by them. I told you—that's how we met—over supporting Barnardo's. But then after Barnardo's, when he was in his late teens he'd fallen in with a bit of a bad lot. That's what he didn't like to talk about. He said it was behind him now, and if Barnardo's had taught him anything, it was that you mustn't let your future be defined by your past."

Cecilia knew about that, too. Michael also had lost his parents when he was young and had an early part of his life that he didn't like to talk about.

"So you don't know who any of the bad lot might be?" Verity said.

"No, I really don't. It was all before we met." She hesitated a moment and then said, "There was one odd thing though—a week or two ago—that I think probably *was* something to do with the past."

The two detectives waited.

"Jack went up to London—I remember exactly now—it was the Thursday before last. He'd paid off the last of his loan on the *Falcon* and he went to the bank to get all the papers from them. Of course we were thrilled we'd paid off the debt and the *Falcon* would be really ours. So we were going to have a little celebration. But then when he got home I could see something was rattling him. So I asked him what was wrong. I thought maybe there'd been a problem at the bank or something. He said no. That was all fine. But then as he was coming back from the bank he'd seen someone in the street he hadn't seen for years and didn't *want* to see again. It quite upset him, he said—which was what I spotted. Anyway, I'm pretty sure that must have been something to with his old lot, the stuff he didn't like to talk about."

"So he didn't mention a name, or anything?"

Adriana shook her head. "I'm pretty sure he didn't. I think I'd remember. It was certainly a man—Jack said 'him' or 'he' a couple of times—and he bumped into him in Millbank—that's where Jack's bank is, or near there. Outside Thames House, I think he said—or maybe it was leaving Thames House. Yes, it was leaving, I'm pretty sure. Does that sound right?"

Cecilia raised an eyebrow. "There's certainly a Thames House in Millbank," she said. "It's the headquarters of MI5."

"Is it? Well, that was where he said."

"And was it that Jack just saw this chap and recognized him?" Verity asked. "Or did they actually speak?"

"Oh, I don't think they spoke. I got the impression Jack saw him and just kept on going."

"Did Jack think the other fellow recognized him?"

"I think he wasn't sure. If he did, it sounded to me as though he didn't want to speak to Jack any more than Jack wanted to speak to him."

Again Verity nodded. "Well, not to worry! Finding out who it might have been, that sort of thing—that's our job." She looked at Cecilia. "Anything else, ma'am?"

Cecilia pulled herself together. "Er—no, I don't think so. Not at the moment. Ms Martínez—Adriana—this must surely be awful for you. Forgive us—but we have to ask these questions."

Adriana Martínez smiled weakly. "I know you do," she said. "And believe me, I'd like you to catch whoever did it, too."

"We'll do our best," Cecilia said.

Verity paused for a moment, gazing at her, then turned back to her neighbour and said, "Adriana, there is one other thing. We did just wonder if Jack had a desk or an office or something where he used to keep papers? There might be something there that would help us."

Cecilia mentally shook her head. She had completely forgotten they were to ask about that.

"Jack had a desk in what he always called his den. Do you want to have a look?"

They went through everything that was to be seen, and found exactly what one would expect—chandler's bills, harbour dues, neatly kept account books with notes of sailings, numbers of passengers and fees paid, tax documents, a folder containing his documents of ownership for the *Falcon*, including final receipts and a letter of congratulation from Culbertson Merchant Bankers in Dean Bradley Street SW1. But they could see nothing that might explain his death.

"This is Jack's handwriting?" Verity asked.

Adriana nodded.

"Then may we keep one of them for the moment, in case we need to compare something else?"

"Yes, of course."

Finally they were ready to leave.

"And if you think of anything," Cecilia said at the front door, "that you think might help—*anything*—well, you know we're here. And you've got DI Jones—Verity—just down the road from you."

"Thank you. I know. You're all being very kind."

Kind? Well, that was something. But hardly what she was there for.

If only she were also alert and on top of things and not merely trying to look like it!

NINE

Pennsylvania, Exeter. The same morning, at about the same time.

Tom Wilkins picked up Headley Harman at the house on Pennsylvania Avenue where he lived with his parents, and they drove out to Topsham together.

Two uniformed officers were waiting for them by the *Falcon*, where they'd been keeping an eye on things since six.

"Anything been happening?" Tom asked.

"Not really. Sam and Annwn last night had a couple of drunks turn up about eleven, and then a false alarm just before one."

"What was that about?"

"They thought they heard a noise from the deck. But they checked and there was no one there. It'll be in their report. Otherwise no one's heard anything. We've been on since six. Just the usual things you'd expect as Topsham woke up, but nothing out of the ordinary. Your arrival's our biggest excitement. That and the smell of someone making coffee."

"So you're going off duty now?"

"Unless you need us."

The two detectives looked at each other.

"Probably not," Tom said. "You chaps go and get some of

that coffee. If we've got a problem and need help we'll call the station."

The two young detectives were used to working together and got on with their task quietly and efficiently. Headley Jarman worked from the bow, and Tom Wilkins from the stern. It was Tom Wilkins who made the discovery, about fifty minutes after they had started.

"Headley, come and look at this! In the main cabin."

He was kneeling at the port side on a bunk that was against the forward cabin wall.

"What's up?"

"Well, I was thinking this cabin was shorter than you'd expect, given the length of the boat."

Headley nodded. That wouldn't have occurred to him, but Tom had an eye for that sort of thing.

"And?"

"It's here. The rest of the wall's solid enough,"—he tapped a part by way of illustration—"but this sounds like ply wood." He tapped again, much nearer the centre. "I'm wondering if—ah!"

He had pushed against it and to the right, and it slid sideways, revealing quite large cavity.

"Ugh. It stinks."

He peered in.

"It's big though!" he said. Then—"Jack Hooper may have been a nice bloke like everyone says, but I think he was smuggling."

"Drugs? Booze?"

"Maybe both. You could carry a load in here. We'd best get forensics back on this. I dare say they can tell. In the meantime"—he reached inside—"there's this."

He pulled out a metal, fireproof document box.

"It's locked," he said after trying it, "But I guess they can open it at the station."

Headley gazed at it for a moment, then looked back at the partition and frowned. "You realize what else you could get in here besides drugs or booze?"

Tom drew in his breath sharply, but then nodded.

"A person? The killer?" he said.

"Right."

"It'd mean he was in there for something like twenty hours."

"Bloody uncomfortable. Cramped. Stuffy. Gruesome. But it's not airtight, and if you had enough motivation—it'd be possible."

Tom nodded. "And it stinks. Whoever it was had to pee, at least once."

"In which case," Headley said, "we've just answered the super's question, 'how did the killer get away?' The killer never left."

"Until HM Coastguard by arrangement with the Devon and Cornwall Constabulary kindly provided a ride home!"

They both chuckled.

"And Sam and Annwn's false alarm last night. I bet it wasn't false at all. Only they'd been told to keep an eye out for people trying to get *on* the boat. No one thought to tell them to look for someone trying to get *off*."

Tom nodded. "We need to call the super about this. If the killer did pee in there, then maybe they can get a DNA sample."

Headley nodded. While urine wasn't the best source for DNA sampling in the world, it was a possible source if it contained any cells. "Maybe they can," he said. "Let's call the super on deck. This whole place is starting to stink."

"I'm for that."

Up on deck they called Cecilia, who sounded pleased with their news and said she would call Foss and forensics.

"And in view of this," she said, "we'd best keep that bit of the *Falcon* as uncontaminated as possible until forensics has gone in again and done its thing. You two keep an eye on it, and I'll get someone from uniform to take over from you as soon as possible."

Their call completed, they walked along the deck on the seaward side of the *Falcon* and peered over. There was a rope hanging down to the water.

"See," Headley said, pointing to it, "the killer could have come up here on deck from the cabin, maybe crashed into something, lost their balance—after hours in that hole you'd be stiff as a board—and then slid down that into the water."

"And then just hung on there, almost out of sight under the lee of the deck, and waited until the coast was clear."

Headley smiled. "Exactly. And in this case, literally."

TEN

St Mary's Rectory, the same morning, about 11.40 a.m.

Michael pulled his car into the vicarage drive, sat back, and sighed.

He'd just spent about an hour with Adriana Martínez. He hoped it had been some use.

When he arrived, she'd offered him tea and he'd accepted.

She brought it to him in a big green and yellow mug, sat down in the chair opposite him and burst into tears.

He passed her a tissue, of which he generally carried a supply, but said nothing. It always seemed to him that Job's comforters did fine just so long as they didn't say anything. It was when they started talking they screwed up.

After a while she looked up at him, tears on her cheeks, and in a choked voice said, "Why?"

"I don't know," he said. "And I'm very sorry."

It wasn't much of an answer, but it was the only honest answer he had.

She nodded.

"No offence to you father, you've always been nice to us. I'm glad you're here. But if God came round at the moment I'd just tell Him to bugger off."

Michael was rather impressed. It took some people a long time to be able to say that.

After a while she began to talk about Jack, and once or twice even laughed through her tears, but finally came back to the tears.

"We were so happy together, I feel as if God played a lousy trick on us—first showed us how nice things can be, and then pushed us off a cliff. I hear all this stuff about how God forgives me for my sins. How about God apologizing to us for what he's done to me and Jack?"

Michael looked at her for a moment, and then decided to take a chance. He began quoting from memory,

> "'My heart is scorched and withered...
> 'Surely I have eaten ashes for bread,
> 'And mingled my drink with tears...
> 'You have taken me up and tossed me aside.'"

She stared at him.

"That's exactly how I feel," she said. "Are you quoting from something?"

"The one hundred and second psalm," he said. "King David telling God to bugger off."

"Oh." Then after a pause, "I never knew there was anything like that in the Bible."

And that, he thought, is because what we serve up on Sundays are mostly the jolly bits.

She then talked more about Jack and their life together, and after a while she let him pray with her and bless her. He always felt enormously privileged when people let him do that.

Finally, as he was about to leave, she said, "Father, I want you to do the funeral. Jack liked you very much, and I know he'd want that. Only I don't know when it can be. They're still doing the post mortem and things—things have to happen—before they'll release him."

He nodded.

"I can enquire about that for you if you like," he said—there were certain advantages in being married to a police officer—"and in any case I'm sure we can fix to do the funeral at a good time for you and have it how you would like."

Which, it occurred to him, was bloody silly way of putting it.

She'd *like* not to be having it at all.

And so now he was back home, somewhat stimulated and somewhat drained, as he always was after such conversations, sitting in his car in the vicarage drive and hoping it had all been some use to her.

The problem—the additional problem, as if sudden and violent death were not problem enough—was that Jack Hooper had been coming to see him on his own over the last few months, and as a result of those visits he knew things about Jack Hooper that he rather thought Adriana Martínez did not know. Neither, for that matter, did Cecilia.

The poor fellow had really been trying to turn his life round. He'd wanted more than anything to ask Adriana to marry him and try for a family. But there were things in his past that he regretted and still worried him, old ties he could not easily escape nor live with easily as a married man. Michael could see that some of those things might have had something to do with his death—and therefore they were things that the police ought to know. And therein lay the dilemma.

On the one hand, Jack hadn't told him all these things in what was formally confession, and Michael hadn't given him formal absolution at the end of it (although he'd considered offering it). If he'd done that, the whole thing would have been subject to the seal of the confessional—the absolute duty of a priest not to disclose anything learnt from a penitent in the Sacrament of Penance.

On the other hand, it had been a pastoral conversation in which secrets had been shared on the clear understanding—in this case, as it happened, explicitly requested by Jack Hooper and agreed to by Michael—that they would never leave his study.

The other side of that, however, was that if something Michael knew might help reveal a man's killer and he didn't reveal it... suppose whoever had killed once killed again? And Michael Aarons' silence was what made that possible?

There was a crackle of tyres on gravel behind him. He looked up and saw with pleasure that the car was Cecilia's, earlier than he'd expected. He'd promised to cook lunch for her and Rosina. His heart grew lighter. That at least was something he could do that was easy and pleasant and involved no moral dilemmas. And he was actually quite good at it!

A few minutes later, after they'd said goodbye to Cecilia's mama who had been baby-sitting, and then greeted Figaro the dog, Rosina their three-year-old daughter, and Felix and Marlene the cats (and if that order seems strange, bear in mind that an enthusiastic dog was always faster than an infant, whereas the cats apparently thought it beneath their dignity to hurry at all: and yet they did show pleasure in their own way, trotting sedately up to Michael with tails upright like masts and writhing round his feet)—after all that had happened, and while Cecilia was setting the table, Michael said, "I had a good visit with Adriana Martínez this morning. At least, I think it was good."

She smiled. "I'm sure it was. I'm glad you went."

"Her grief is real," he said. "I'm sure of that." That much, at least, he felt he could reveal, since it was as much as anything a comment about his own feelings.

She looked up from straightening a napkin and met his eye. "Thank you. I think so too."

ELEVEN

Heavitree Police Station: that afternoon.

The team gathered in Cecilia's office at three, as planned. Despite it being obvious that both she and Michael had much on their minds, Cecilia had enjoyed her lunch with him and Rosina, and had taken a nap with Rosina after it. As a result, she was feeling brighter.

She had the meeting begin with sharing information they'd gathered that morning from their different routes of enquiry. She started with Tom and Headley's discoveries aboard the *Falcon*, then turned to her and Verity's conversation with Adriana Martínez. Somewhat to her surprise, covering this took the best part of an hour. She looked at the clock and shook her head. Why is it that everything always takes longer than you think it will?

"Let's take a break," she said.

Everyone got more coffee—which in Cecilia's office was now quite decent, as a result of her providing her own beans, her own grinder, and her own coffeemaker. When they'd regrouped, she proceeded to Joseph's researches into Jack Hooper and Adriana Martínez.

"Your turn, Joseph. Show us what you've got!"

"Right. Well Adriana Martínez seems pretty straightforward. Of course the family background on her dad's side is Spanish—Adriana's great grandfather was on the losing side in the Spanish Civil War and fled to England in 1939. But after three generations I think the family's pretty well gone native. Father and mother both lawyers—that's how they met, working in the same chambers in London. Adriana has one elder brother. He's in the army, major in the Queen's Royal Hussars. Served in Afghanistan, something of a hero, Military Cross. Adriana went to Cheltenham Ladies College, and then on to Exeter University."

Cecilia immediately wondered whether her papa had ever had Adriana in a class?

"She read English," Joseph continued.

Ah—then probably not. Papa taught classics.

"She wasn't a brilliant student, but she wasn't a bad one either: graduated with a solid second. So far as I can tell, she was popular. She also showed something of a social conscience and was generally into good works. She went on outreach trips with the university to places like the West Indies and South America to help with poverty: helping to build decent housing, that sort of thing."

Cecilia now knew exactly how papa would describe her: "doubtless an excellent citizen though never a profound scholar."

"She did an extra year in London at City University studying for a postgraduate degree in Library Science, came back here, and took a job in the University Library. She's been here ever since. So far as I can see she's well liked, good at her job and in line for promotion. She and Jack met while she was an undergraduate but nothing came of it. Then they linked up again after she came back to Exeter from her year in London and they've been steady ever since. They took a house together four years ago: joint ownership, mortgage, everything proper."

He looked up and smiled. "In other words, if there's anything odd or suspicious about Adriana Martínez, I haven't found it."

He turned to another set of notes on his iPad.

"Now, her partner Jack Hooper. He's quite a different kettle of fish. Born in the East End of London, orphaned when he was five, brought up by Barnardo's, and did well, though definitely a practical chap rather than an academic."

"A man what can and what does," Verity said.

"Exactly. He left when he was eighteen and got a job in a meat packing plant. Then things started to go pear-shaped. Not to take too long over it, he fell in with a nasty little lot, neo-Nazis and really violent. Eventually but pretty dreadfully they got their come-uppance after they'd started a fire in the house of a Jewish family who'd annoyed them. It got out of hand and six people died. Unluckily for them, and luckily for everyone else, various people spotted them putting the petrol bomb through the letterbox, and although the place went up like tinder and no one could do anything to save the people in it, they were at least nabbed by the police and charged—multiple charges of criminal manslaughter. All of them got hefty sentences—life without parole—all that is except young Jack Hooper, who was heard by several witnesses arguing with the gang members who were about to put the bomb in and trying to dissuade them from it. That saved him. He was much younger than the others, of course. Anyway, he got off with three months for aiding and abetting, of which he served two.

"When he'd finished that, he seems to have decided after a few months that he'd had enough of the big city. He came down here to the West Country where he got various jobs, and more and more of those jobs involved crewing and sailing, for which he obviously found he had a taste and a knack. In 2007 he gained his master's certificate and invested in his own boat, the *Falcon*, which he's been using to earn a living with ever since. He finally paid off his loan on that a couple of weeks ago—we've seen the documentation and the bank confirm his going in to sign the final papers, just as

Adriana says he did. There's more to say about what he's actually been *doing* with the boat, as we'll see when we get to the box that Tom and Headley found, but I'll leave that until then. I'll just say apropos the sailing that he is generally regarded as an excellent small boat sailor. I'll email you all copies of my notes with dates and places and things on both of them, but that's the gist of what I've found so far. Any questions?"

There were none, only general murmurs of "great job, Joseph" and "I don't know how you do it"—to which Joseph gave his usual reply—"It's nothing that couldn't be managed by any obsessive compulsive with access to the Internet."

"I do have one question," Cecilia said. "I'd like to know more about the gang he was in—especially the people who were with him that night. Who were they all? What's happened to them? And especially, where are they now? I'd also like to know about the people in the house they burned down. Did anyone survive? Were they part of a larger family? If so, then where are they now?"

Joseph grinned. "That's several questions, ma'am!"

Cecilia chuckled. "Right!"

"I'll get onto it."

Cecilia turned next to the enquiries that Verity had instigated by uniformed officers in and around Topsham Quay. These had been by no means fruitless. Two people on neighbouring vessels independently said on the night of the murder they'd seen someone go on board the *Falcon* who wasn't Jack Hooper, whom they both knew and were pretty sure they would have recognized. Both said whoever-it-was was too short to be Jack Hooper. And both said there were already lights on in the Falcon's cabin, so they'd assumed Jack was already on board.

Beyond that, however, their descriptions of the unknown visitor weren't much use. They'd pointed out that it had been "getting dark" or was already "pretty dark". One of them thought the visitor was wearing a hoody, though he wasn't sure. Neither of them had taken any notice of the time: "some time after nine-thirty" and "maybe ten-ish" were the best either of them could do.

"What about CCTV?" Tom said. "Is the quay covered?"

"Yes and no," Joseph said. "It's covered in theory. Unfortunately for us the camera covering the bit where the *Falcon* was parked is out. And the one covering the way people go onto the quay is very blurred. You can see people coming and going round about nine-thirty but nothing you can really make out. So it's pretty useless. And no doubt most of them were just going to the pub."

Cecilia shook her head. CCTV is fine, but like everything else it needs maintenance. And budget cuts meant maintenance wasn't happening. Damn!

Nevertheless, they had enough for Verity to get up from her chair, take the marker and solemnly sketch on the whiteboard, next to photographs of the victim and others involved in the murder, an outline figure with no face and a curl on its head that might have been a question mark.

Cecilia turned next to Tom Foss's evidence, which he'd sent to her earlier that afternoon. He had made two further interesting discoveries. First, forensic examination at the laboratory had revealed not only bruising on the victim's knuckles but also traces of blood—blood that wasn't the victim's.

"It looks," she said, "as though Hooper hit his killer hard enough at least once to draw blood. So—we're looking for a killer who perhaps has the marks of a fight on him—a split lip or some-thing like that—and more importantly, once the blood we found on Hooper has been checked, we should have the killer's DNA."

The others nodded.

"Next," she continued, "there's the hidey-hole on the *Falcon*. Foss did find traces of urine in there, just as you'd hoped." She nodded acknowledgement to Headley and Tom. "Both the blood and the urine are being checked as we speak. Assuming we get DNA samplings from either or both, of course we'll compare them to all the databases and see if they ID our killer for us."

This was good. And there was more to come.

Verity had a penchant (which she happily admitted came from her childhood) for saving the best bit until last, and Cecilia noted with amusement that it was certainly her influence on the agenda that led them only last of all to the contents of the fireproof box that Tom and Headley had found on the *Falcon*. It turned out that it contained a ledger, and the ledger contained a handwritten business record of supplies delivered, meticulously detailed with dates, quantities and prices, going back several years. It was the same handwriting as the account ledgers in Jack Hooper's desk.

"And it's all about wine," Joseph said. "Good quality French wine, and some French brandy: all of it medium to high end. In other words, he was helping to make ends meet and pay off the loan on his boat by smuggling."

"Just wine and brandy? What about tobacco? Drugs?" Tom asked.

"Actually, no. Tom Foss says there's absolutely no evidence the *Falcon* has ever carried either—and he reckons he'd find it if she had. He had a sniffer dog this afternoon check out the whole vessel, including the secret space. He says it's impossible to hide drugs from a trained dog, or where they've been stored. But the only thing the Falcon appears to have carried is booze. Which, given the size of that hold, and the number of shipments in the ledger, meant a nice little earner on the side for him—seven or eight hundred pounds every time he did it, I'd say."

"Nice, as you say—but not exactly enormous," Tom said. "He could much make more than that hauling tobacco and ten times more than that hauling drugs."

"So he wasn't above making a bit on the side, but not exactly a lord of crime?"

"Exactly. Judging by the ledger he had a convenient little setup with one person. All of the cargoes seem to be designated for someone called 'C'—and thanks to a card that may have got stuck in the ledger by accident, it also looks as though we know who 'C' is. Carter's Wine, store and warehouse in Princesshay."

"Oh my! Definitely high end," Verity said.

Joseph smiled. "The owner of the business is a fellow called Richard Carter. He has a rather large and splendid house in Topsham, as it happens. And a yacht! Here is a photograph of him"—he handed a photograph to Cecilia, which she looked at and then passed to the others—"He's a hundred and seventy two centimetres tall—five foot seven and a half inches. Quite short. In other words, he fits the description, such as we have, of someone boarding the *Falcon* on the night of the murder."

There was a pause.

"Adriana Martínez said she was surprised at how profitable Jack's boat business was," Cecilia said. "I suppose now we know why."

"Was she really as innocent as that? Or did she know how he was making extra money?"

Cecilia shrugged. "So far at least there's no evidence she knew. Unless and until we find evidence, I'll give her the benefit of the doubt."

"Then again," Headley said, "smuggling booze is a classic form of west country employment. People have been doing it for centuries."

"That's right," Tom said. "As a matter of fact there was another fellow called Carter doing it way back in the seventeen hundreds. John Carter. He was really good at it. Made a fortune."

"Wait a minute," Joseph said, "I think I've heard of him. Isn't he the chap that had everyone face the wall while they brought the booze into the village? So afterwards they could truthfully tell the excise men they hadn't seen anything?"

"That's right," said Tom, adding in his best Devon accent,

"Watch the wall, my darling, while the gentlemen go by!
"Them that asks no questions, they ain't told no lie."

"There you are—sounds like it's the family business," Headley said.

There was a general chuckle.

"There's one other thing that strikes me about this record," Verity said, peering at the ledger.

The others looked at her.

"The last shipment," she said. "It's dated at the end of last month, and there are three lines under it, with a note 'Final delivery.' No other delivery is marked like that. And there are no deliveries in the ledger *after* that."

"Are you suggesting Hooper was actually planning to *stop* smuggling?" Cecilia asked.

"Either that, or at least to stop smuggling for Carter's Wine. Maybe he'd had a better offer."

"And someone might get mad at him about that."

"They might."

"Mad enough to kill him?"

"Maybe," Verity said.

Cecilia nodded. It was possible. Logic might point out that the ending of an arrangement that involved at most a few hundred pounds a month was a poor motive for someone as well off as Richard Carter to kill someone. But then, logic didn't always govern how people acted. Think of Othello! And in any case, there was plenty of evidence here of criminal activity.

She sat back in her chair and surveyed the group.

"For several reasons," she said, "not all of them directly connected with our murder, we obviously need to take a look inside Carter's Wine and especially their warehouse. I think I'd better go and see the chief super now."

The others nodded.

If they were going to look inside Carter's Wine they would need a search warrant. For that they would need to approach a magistrate. And for *that* they would need the Chief Superintendent to agree.

TWELVE

G lyn Davies was entirely amenable.

"You've certainly got a case for a warrant," he said to Cecilia after she'd explained the team's findings so far. "I happen to know Sir John Hull's in the city. I'll get on to him."

She nodded. That would be fine. She knew Sir John slightly, and had appeared before him once or twice. A stickler for the law, which was his job (as Glyn Davies invariably pointed out), but always fair.

"We'll need to search Carter's Wine *and* Richard Carter's home," the chief superintendent continued, "in case he's got the incriminating stuff there. We should do the searches simultaneously. We'll need warrants to cover both."

Cecilia nodded. "Sounds good."

"It's your case, Cecilia so do as you think best, but assuming we get the warrants, I do have a suggestion."

"Sir?"

"Since your main concern is your murderer, and Carter is looking like a suspect, why don't you and Verity lead the group at his home and deal with him? I could lead the group at the warehouse for you."

"Good idea, sir. Let's do that."

She really did think it was a good idea, although knowing Glyn Davies, she suspected he was also enjoying the prospect of a little police work that didn't involve sitting behind his desk or being in a meeting.

A special sitting of the magistrate's court was convened in the judge's chambers for 7.00 pm. Present were Sir John Hull himself, together with a clerk to the court, the Chief Superintendent, and a lawyer from the Crown Prosecution Service. Cecilia was also there to present her team's evidence and their reasons for supposing that crimes had been and were in the process of being committed on the premises they wished to investigate, and that the owners of said premises probably would not willingly cooperate with a police investigation.

The business did not take long. The judge listened attentively to their presentations, from time to time making notes, had a brief word with his clerk, then declared himself satisfied.

"This certainly justifies investigation," he said. "Chief Superintendent, Detective Superintendent, you have your warrants."

"Let's get on with this," Glyn Davies said to Cecilia as soon as the hearing was over. "How long do you need to organize?"

"A couple of hours at most," she said.

"Good. Then let's say we go in at ten."

Cecilia swallowed a smile. Here was a man who was definitely looking forward to a spot of action!

But, "Yes, sir," was all that she said.

Thirteen

Ted Marple, night watchman at Carter's Wine in Princesshay, put four spoonsful of sugar into his tea, stirred it, tasted it, added two more spoonsful, stirred it again, tasted it again and nodded with satisfaction. He left the small room with the electric kettle in it—virtually a cupboard—and took his mug of tea to the cubbyhole where he had an armchair and a wooden box that served as a table. Here, between the store closing at nine and opening again at eight, he generally spent whatever time there was when he was not, in his capacity as nightwatchman, patrolling the building.

He had just seated himself comfortably with his tea and had fished out of his khaki pack an enormous sausage and bacon butty, when the main doorbell rang from the front of the shop.

It always seemed louder when the place was empty.

"Sod it," he said to himself.

It was a bit earlier than usual, but all England to a postage stamp it was some idiot boozed out of his mind.

The bell rang again.

"Sod it," he said again, this time aloud. "S'pose I'd better go and see."

Carefully placing his mug of tea and his butty on the box beside his chair, he got to his feet and made his way slowly through the warehouse past stacks of crates, cartons and boxes to the shop at the front of the building, which faced onto Princesshay.

By the time he got three quarters of the way, the bell had rung again, and as he entered the shop it rang a fourth time.

"All right, all right," he said. "I'm bloody coming, are'n I?"

The beams of powerful LED torches were shining in through the plate glass of the entrance door and the large display windows, flashing round shelves and the counters, after a moment picking him up as he made his way toward the door.

The ringing stopped.

There were people outside the door waiting for him to open it. A lot of people.

"Christ!" he said. Princesshay is well lit, especially where the expensive shops are, and he could now see that the waiting people weren't drunks at all. They were the police, and beyond them a few late evening walkers watching curiously. Christ, what the shit did they want?

He arrived at the door and opened it clumsily, for his hands were sweating.

"Good evening, sir," said the policeman facing him. "I am Chief Superintendent Davies, Exeter CID. Who are you?"

He looked important. There was silver braid on the peak of his cap.

"I'm Ted Marple, sir. I'm the night watchman here."

"Well Mr Marple, I have a warrant to search these premises, so I must ask you to step aside and let us in."

Ted Marple was not a man to argue with any policeman, and especially not one with silver braid on his cap.

He stepped aside.

FOURTEEN

Topsham. Richard Carter's house.
At about the same time.

"Look where you like," Richard Carter said when Cecilia and Verity and their team arrived and he'd seen the warrant.

Which immediately led Cecilia to suspect he knew there was nothing incriminating in the house. Still, he might be bluffing. So the team went in anyway.

"You're wasting your time, you know."

She eyed him speculatively. He was small of stature, confident, and some would have said quite good-looking, although running a little to flab. He had a plaster on his forehead, which looked to be covering a small cut. She already disliked him, though she wasn't sure why.

Her mobile phone buzzed. It was Glyn Davies.

"Well, we'll have to see if we're wasting our time, won't we, Mr Carter?" she said. "In the meantime excuse me, I need to take this."

She left him with Verity Jones and the uniformed search team, and walked into the next room. Glyn Davies sounded as though he was enjoying himself.

"We've found three batches of wine and brandy on which duty

has clearly not been paid. One batch appears to correspond exactly to the last transaction listed in Hooper's ledger, but it looks as if Carter's also using at least one other small supplier—maybe even two—in the same way as he uses Hooper. Altogether, it's going to add up to quite an amount."

"Right."

"We'll need," Glyn Davies continued, "to hand over this aspect of things to HMRC"—that was, Her Majesty's Revenue and Customs—"and I dare say they'll be involving Border Force and the French Customs too. I know that your concern is the murder, but maybe your knowing about all this will help you shake him up generally."

"Got it!"

As Cecilia was putting away her mobile, Verity entered the room.

"So far there's nothing here that's obviously incriminating. We've done the whole house, including the attic. The papers in the desk seem to be fairly routine household bills and such, but we're taking them all and his computer, just in case."

"All right. The good news is, the chief super and his lot have had much more success at the warehouse. There's a mass of stuff that's never had duty paid on it."

Verity nodded. "That's more like it."

"Now, where's Carter?"

Verity grinned. "He's in his study, complaining."

"Is he? Well, let's go and give him something to complain about, shall we?"

FIFTEEN

Carter's study, a few minutes later.

Carter was standing by his desk. Actually, at this moment he wasn't complaining. He was smiling. Cecilia was surer than ever that she didn't like him.

"Well," he said. "I told you there was nothing here. I can't imagine what you think you're going to find among those household bills your sergeant's taken—or on the computer, beyond my wife's emails and the short story my daughter's writing on it."

"Probably not a lot, Mr Carter. We just thought there might be a note or two about your bootlegged wine and brandy."

"There is no bootlegged wine."

"Oh, really? What about all the stuff that my colleagues have just found in your warehouse? Several batches, I gather. A nice little profit for you there."

He shrugged. "All right. You've got me. So what's the search about? Do you think I keep the stuff at home too? And implicate my family?"

"I've no idea, and anyway, that's not really a matter for me. You'll have to deal with HM Customs and Excise and the courts over that. And I gather these days they're being pretty tough. No,

what I'd like to talk to you about is Jack Hooper. A friend of yours,
I think?"

"Jack Hooper? Yes, I know him. What about him?"

"Old friends are you, sir?"

"I've known him a while."

"And when did you last see him?"

"We see each other on and off."

Evading the question.

"And when was the last time?"

"I'm not sure I remember."

"Well let me jog your memory. Would it help if I told you we
have a witness that saw you boarding Hooper's boat during the
late evening the night before last?"

She really wasn't sure that the witnesses they had would
actually pick him out in a line-up, but they might. Carter himself,
however, resolved her uncertainty.

"Oh, yes, I suppose that's right. I did see him then."

Well, that was easy enough.

"And what did you talk about?"

"I don't really remember. This and that."

She looked at Verity, who shook her head, and smiled at him.

"Really, sir," she said, "you aren't helping yourself by wasting
our time. We've seen Hooper's records. We know he was supplying you with wine and brandy. Indeed, we know precisely how
much he was supplying you with. It's hard to believe you didn't
talk about that."

He shook his head and looked resigned. "All right so he's been
supplying me. But he's stopped now. He wants to get out of it. It's
this girl he lives with. She wouldn't like it if she found out about it,
so he wants to stop."

"And when did he tell you all this?"

"A couple of weeks' back, when I took the last delivery."

"So why did you go to see him the night before last?"

"To make sure he hadn't changed his mind. Basically, I like dealing with the man. He's straight and he's reliable, which is more than you can say for a lot of people in this trade. And I wanted to make sure he knew he could always come back in if he wanted to."

"And did he?"

"No. He was quite clear. He's done with it."

"So what happened then?"

"What happened then was I wished him well and I pushed off."

"Did you really? Pushed off where?"

"Down to the shack."

Cecilia and Verity stared at him.

"We've a little place on the estuary near where we keep the boat. We always call it 'the shack'. Sophie and Jenny—that's my wife and our daughter—are staying with her mother in Normandy and the house is empty. So I'd decided to spend the night in the shack and then be up early and go out fishing on the *Swan*. That's our boat. The storm delayed me going out a bit, but not much."

"So you're a competent sailor?" Cecilia put in.

"Have been for years," he said. "My dad and I sailed out to Bermuda once."

She raised and eyebrow, but said nothing.

"And that's what you did?" Verity said. "Went fishing all day in your boat?"

"Yes."

"Alone?"

"Yes, of course."

"You were alone the whole time?"

"I just told you. Yes."

"And then what?"

"I got in about nine that night, went home, made some supper, ate it and went to bed."

"So you still didn't see anyone?"

"No. Why? Look, you've obviously got all the evidence you need. What does it matter if I went fishing?"

"We've got all the evidence we need about the smuggled wines and brandy," Cecilia said.

He shrugged. "So then—I'm nicked. The wine and brandy will be confiscated and maybe the truck we picked it up in from the *Falcon* will be confiscated too, and I dare say I'll have to pay a hell of a fine. And maybe I'll get gaol, though with luck a decent lawyer will get me off that. What more do you want?"

He's good, she thought. He really looks as though he doesn't know.

"What do you think has happened to Jack Hooper?" she said.

He looked puzzled. "From what you've told me, I suppose you've arrested him for smuggling. But I'm telling you he really was trying to stop it. He was getting out. That ought to count for something in his favour."

"Haven't you seen the news lately?"

He looked more puzzled than ever. "The news? What news?"

"The news. On television."

"Never watch it. It's all cuts and Brexit and Greasy-Mogg and boring Boris whining like spoiled schoolboys and I find it just too bloody depressing."

Well, she could sympathize with that.

"Why did you try to avoid my question when I asked you if you'd been to see Jack Hooper?" she asked.

"I'd have thought that was bloody obvious. You're onto the contraband booze and as I keep telling you Jack was trying to get out of it. I didn't want to implicate him if I didn't have to. Okay, so he's not above making a bob or so on the side, but he's a decent man. But then—well, it's obvious you've found all the evidence against him anyway, so it doesn't make any difference whether I talked to him or not, does it?"

Cecilia sighed. "And after you talked to him, you just left him?"

"As I keep telling you. I doubt I was there more than ten minutes. There was a storm coming on, and he wanted to get on with making sure everything was secure. So I asked him if he wanted any help and he said he was fine and he'd almost finished, and I left him to it."

"And that's it?"

"That's it."

"How did you get that cut on your forehead, Mr Carter?"

"What cut? Oh, that. Banged it on the medicine chest door in the bathroom. My wife keeps telling me to get it fixed. Look, why are you harping on about this?"

"Because Jack Hooper was murdered at between 9.30 and 10.30 on the evening when you went to see him."

"*What?*"

There was a pause.

"Jesus Christ," he said quietly.

She had to admit he looked genuinely stunned. Even appalled. And yet... there were too many coincidences here to ignore.

"I put it to you," she said quietly, "that you were angry about Hooper's stopping supplying you, that you went to see him and had an argument about it that turned into a fight. It all went further than you intended and—perhaps accidentally—you killed him. You then decided that you must make it look like an accident in the storm. You took the *Falcon* out to sea—you are, as you say, a very competent sailor—you arranged the body to look like an accident, and then hid on the *Falcon* until there was a convenient moment to make your getaway."

"But—but—that's terrible. I keep telling you, Jack Hooper was fine when I left him. How can you possibly believe I did it? I *like* the man... liked him."

"I suppose, Mr Carter, I can believe you did it because I find it so hard to believe the alternative. If you didn't do it I have to believe it's just coincidence Jack Hooper was murdered aboard his vessel a very short while—a half hour at most—after you were seen boarding it, and at a time when you clearly had reason to be angry with him. I have to believe it's just coincidence that Hooper evidently put up a fight and you have a cut that looks exactly as though you've been in a fight. Finally, I have to believe it's also just coincidence that while you evidently *do* have the skills needed to do what Jack Hooper's killer did—to take his boat out to sea and then ride out the storm—you *don't* an alibi for the time those things happened and the following *twenty-four hours*—which is a long time in which to be seen by no one!—in other words, you've no alibi for precisely the period when Jack Hooper's killer had to hide out on the *Falcon*."

Carter stood staring at her.

"Well then," he said finally, "are you going to arrest me for murder or what? Since it's obvious you don't believe a word I say."

She paused. The coincidences involved in his story *were* hard to believe, but they weren't actually impossible. And what did she always say was one of the principles of sound detective work? What we can't show, we don't know.

She sighed.

"All right," she said finally, "your story, though unlikely, just might be true. So for the present I'm going to have you arrested for alcohol fraud, of which we have clear evidence. The more serious charge can wait. Detective Inspector, will you charge Mr Carter and caution him?"

"Ma'am."

"Can I call my solicitor?" he said.

"Of course you can."

"Should I cuff him, ma'am?" Verity said.

Cecilia looked at him. Arresting officers in the United Kingdom may use their discretion in choosing whether or not to handcuff a person in custody, and she'd never been one to impose humiliation where it wasn't necessary.

"Will you come quietly?" she said.

He gave the ghost of a smile. "Do I have a choice?"

Despite herself, she found herself giving the ghost of smile in return. "Not really."

"Then I'll come quietly."

She nodded to Verity. "No need for cuffs, then."

Cecilia walked to the door and thence through the spacious hall to the front door, where she stood out on the porch looking over the estuary. She took a deep breath. The sky was clear. There was a waning moon and stars reflected in the Exe, which now ran calm and quiet as if no storm had ever disturbed it. A church clock chimed from somewhere, echoing over the water. She looked at her watch. Just on eleven. How much had happened in an hour! She supposed she ought to be satisfied: they definitely had a result, and very possibly two. But for some reason she felt empty—tired and empty.

Even the moon looked wan and pale.

Verity joined her after uniformed officers had led Richard Carter away

"He acts," she said, "very much as though he really didn't know Jack Hooper was dead. I find him rather convincing. If he isn't innocent, he's a good actor."

"I know," Cecilia said, frowning.

Verity was right. Carter *did* sound convincing. But then, there were all those coincidences... and *one may smile and smile, and be a villain.*

"Let's remember," she said, "we do have, or should soon have, DNA of Jack Hooper's killer. And since we've arrested him, we can have Carter's DNA, too. Then we'll know whether he's telling us the truth or not."

It would also help, she reflected, if we had another credible witness.

SIXTEEN

Heavitree Police Station, the following day, Friday, 7th September.

The following morning, and as if to prove the truth of the adage, "be careful what you pray for," it turned out they *did* have another credible witness. Uniformed officers making enquiries along the estuary came up with a local sailor who had himself been planning to go fishing on the morning after the storm, who knew Carter quite well by sight, and had noticed him preparing his vessel.

No, he hadn't actually spoken to him, but he was pretty sure it was Carter and he was certain it was Carter's vessel.

If the witness was right, this went some way toward confirming the story Carter had told Cecilia and Verity, and all the way toward confirming that he couldn't possibly at the same time have been hiding on the *Falcon*, seven or so miles out at sea.

If the witness was right... "pretty sure" is not, however, "dead certain", and the final coup de grâce to Cecilia's theories did not come until half an hour or so later when the phone on her desk flashed.

It was Tom Foss.

"We just got results of the DNA test on Carter," he said brightly.

"And the lab was also able to get a DNA sample from the urine in *Falcon*."

"That was quick," she said. These days getting DNA results could take days, and at times weeks.

"It was, but you're not going to like it. It *was* the same person who had a punch up with Jack Hooper and then relieved himself in the hidey-hole on the *Falcon*." He paused. "But it wasn't Richard Carter."

"Damn," she said. "I really hoped it would be him."

"Well it isn't. But it *is* someone who's on the Europol Database."

"Go on."

"He's called Marcel Gagnon: half-French, half English, broken home, grew up in England with his father and younger brother Armand. His father skippered yachts for a living so he was raised around boats and he's spent a lot of time crewing—in other words, he knows how to sail. Interestingly enough, his hiding out on the *Falcon* isn't the first time he's pulled a stunt like that. He evaded capture by French police a couple of years back in much the same way. He hid in a culvert for fifteen hours. It never occurred to anyone that a fully grown man could even get into the thing, let alone stick it out that long! Aside from all that, he's clearly a thug who's willing to kill when paid for it. He's wanted in connection with two other murders. Obviously he's not an entirely successful assassin or he wouldn't be on the database. Equally obviously he's a nasty piece of work."

Cecilia shook her head. What was it Commander Salmon used to say? Professional killers are like plumbers and electricians: people are always trying to find a good one.

SEVENTEEN

Heavitree Police Station, later the same day.

"So," Cecilia said when the team gathered in her office that afternoon, "we've issued a European Arrest Warrant for Marcel Gagnon. As it happens, there are two other warrants out for him already, so if anyone does find him I dare say we'll have to wait in line."

"And is that it?" Tom asked. "We just wait?"

"Not at all," Cecilia said. "Gagnon's a mercenary, an assassin for hire. That's obvious. And of course we want him caught. But what I really want to find out is who hired him. I want to catch the *real* killer. We're going to have to dig deeper."

"Which means, I suppose, that Carter isn't entirely out of the frame," Joseph said. "Maybe he paid this Gagnon fellow to do it."

"And then carefully *didn't* provide himself with a proper alibi?" Verity said.

"Maybe he knew Gagnon would do it, but not when," Tom said.

Cecilia shook her head. "We're snatching at straws. Yes, in theory it might still be Carter, and I admit I hoped it would be. But as Verity pointed out before I had the gumption to admit it,

Carter's actually a rather convincing witness in his own defence. And the only independent witness we have goes some way to supporting his story. We have to cast our net wider."

"So what about those nasty people Jack Hooper got mixed up with when he was young and foolish?" Headley said. "Shouldn't we be taking a look at them?"

"I agree," Cecilia said. "Joseph, you were going to do some research on them?"

"I was," Joseph said, "and I have."

They looked at him expectantly.

"In a way," he said, "there isn't a lot to tell. There were four of them: two brothers, George and Arthur Williams, and two other fellows, Samuel Slater and William Craig. The Williams brothers and Slater were hard men: various counts of assault and grievous bodily harm. They were also extreme right wing activists—neo-Nazis—in the National Front and then the British National Party for a bit, but apparently even those were too liberal for them, and they left and joined the British Union."

"I don't think I've heard of that."

"Well you can visit their website if you've nothing better to do. It's vile: anti-Jewish, anti-Moslem, homophobic and anti-coloured of course. They press every button. Anyway, after the fire the Williams brothers and Slater were arrested, and they got life. Slater was a little older than the others and died a couple of years ago, but the Williams are both alive and still in gaol."

Being in gaol did not, of course, necessarily mean that one was incapable of organizing a crime outside of gaol. It all depended on who you knew and what you knew.

"And the other one—the fourth one? What do we know about him?"

"Craig, yes. He seems to have been different. He was wealthy and better educated: went to Eton—a King's Scholar, which I gather means he was intelligent—"

"*Very* intelligent," Verity said. "There are only fourteen of them each year. It's a big thing."

The others looked at her.

"I had a boyfriend who was a King's Scholar," she said. "Read PPE and got a first."

Cecilia smiled inwardly. Verity had graduated with a double first, though she never mentioned it.

"Okay, *very* intelligent!" Joseph said. "He was set to go to Oxford. Had a place at Christ Church, but he never took it up."

"Really? Why was that?"

Joseph shook his head. "I guess he'd got mixed up with this right wing lot, and wanted to spend his time politicking. Anyway, following the firebombing he disappeared. They traced his tracks as far as Dover, where he seems to have got on a cross-channel ferry. He was spotted in Paris. There's a sighting on AutoRoute E35 and a possible sighting on the A2 near Lucerne. Then nothing. That's the end. So far I can find nothing else about him at all. National Insurance, credit cards, all the usual things—nothing. If he's still alive then somehow he, or someone he's in cahoots with, has covered his tracks amazingly well. Maybe someone's given him a new identity. For the moment I just don't know."

There was a pause.

Cecilia sighed. For Joseph, this was unusual indeed.

"Right, then," she said finally, "so I suppose we just have to keep looking. Or rather you do!"

He grinned and nodded.

"Back to the Williams brothers," she continued. "You said they were in gaol. Where?"

"Belmarsh."

She nodded. HM Prison Belmarsh, a Category A men's prison in Thamesmead, southeast London. She knew it slightly, and had visited it once.

"Verity," she said, "you and I need to call on them. I'd like to see their reactions to Hooper's death face to face. Will you talk to the prison about arranging that? Soon."

Verity nodded. "On it, ma'am."

"Next, what about the people whose house was burned. Who were they? Who died and more importantly, who didn't?"

Joseph nodded. "They were a family called Heschel. It was dreadful. A couple in their late twenties—Joseph and Esther—their two young children, Samuel and Miriam, aged three and five, and Esther's parents, Tobias and Miriam, in their fifties: all died in the fire or shortly afterwards from burns. The only survivor was Joseph and Esther's third son, also called Tobias, aged seven. And he survived because he was away from the house that night, staying for a sleepover with his cousins in their home in Golders Green."

"And where is he now?"

"He's one of the artistic directors' team at the Covent Garden Opera."

"Then we need to see him too. Verity? Maybe you and I can manage them all in the same day?"

Again Verity nodded. "I'll fix it."

EIGHTEEN

Exeter, outside St Leonard's School. About half an hour later.

Cecilia left early so she was able to go with Michael to pick up Rachel from school.

"Ah, there she is!"

Rachel was standing with a slightly plump girl who was wearing spectacles—but as soon as she saw Michael and Cecilia and the car she left the girl and ran across to them.

"Who's your friend?" Cecilia asked when she got in. "I don't think I've seen her before?"

"Who? Oh, *that*! That's Tabitha Timms. She's new this term and she's *very* stupid and annoying."

"How is she stupid and annoying?"

"She follows me around in the playground and then she goes and sits by me at lunch."

"That sounds to me like someone who's trying to be friends," Michael said.

"Well she's stupid."

"Because she wants to be friends with you?" he said mildly.

"She's got glasses and frizzy hair and spots."

"They look like freckles to me," he said.

"Whatever."

"In other words," Cecilia said, "she's different from you and your friends."

"Yes."

"Have you talked to her?"

"No, of course not."

Cecilia gazed speculatively at their gorgeous, precocious, self-confident daughter, who at eight years old feared nothing and was undoubtedly a queen already in her own world, a ruling member among the bright and beautiful, with no time at all for frizzy-haired and freckled people with glasses who weren't lucky enough to be like her.

There flashed before her a moment in her own school life: her thirteen-year-old self, newly transferred to a different class, smaller than everyone else and darker than everyone else, dismissed by all as "the little dago" and desperate for a friend.

And then there had been Arethusa Stone, older than she and larger than she. Arethusa Stone declared loudly and scornfully, "all Italians are cowards." So Cecilia flew at her and fought her and was knocked down, and got up and fought her and was knocked down again, and got up again and fought her again, time after time refusing to stay down, until at last, bruised and bloody, she was dragged bodily from the fracas by her form-mistress who declared as she did it, "You know what your trouble is, Cavaliere? You don't seem to know when you're beaten!"

They'd treated her better after that. Even Arethusa Stone! She'd won respect. And then later in her teens she'd shot up and become tall and strong and beautiful, as sometimes happens, and they'd all had to look up to her—literally.

But could it be that she and Michael were now raising a new Arethusa Stone, who must be fought before she would give you respect? Was that how it always had to be? She felt she should say something. But she was not at all sure what.

"You know," Michael said, "Figaro was the runt of the litter when mama got him. All the other puppies were bigger than he was and he couldn't get much food."

"Figaro's the best dog in the world!"

"I know he is. But he got like that because mama was nice to him."

"I don't see what that's got to do with me and Tabitha Timms."

"Don't you?" he said as he slid the car into drive. "Are you sure?"

NINETEEN

"Certainly real men cry," papa had said to Cecilia one day when she was little and they were discussing some ancient battle where the victors had shed tears over the slain and she had expressed surprise. All those hoary toughs in armour weeping and hugging each other? That was surely absurd.

But of course papa had been right, and today she'd seen it. They'd interviewed the Williams brothers separately. Prison life, though severe, was doubtless healthy enough, especially for a hard man—Belmarsh, to be sure, had in its time had something of a reputation for intimidation—and both brothers, muscular and heavily tattooed, while clearly no longer young, looked lean and fit. They were doubtless well able to handle themselves. Each, however, seemed genuinely sorry to learn of Jack Hooper's death, and to her surprise the elder, George Williams, openly wept.

"Jack was a good lad," he said. "I hope you get the piece of shit that did it."

"Yet Jack did get off a big sentence when you and your brother went down," Verity said. "You must have been a bit angry about that."

"At the time?" He shook his head. "Yeah, maybe I was pissed off at the time. But I've thought about it a lot since. Firebombing that family! There were kids in there, and Jack saw it. We were just doing it because they were Jews. Jews, Muslims, coloureds, they were the villains. We didn't know or care a fucking thing about who we hurt."

"What had you against Jews?" Cecilia asked, thinking of Michael.

He gave a grim laugh. "Fuck all! I knew about as much about Jews as I know about... about Eskimos. But we used to read all those websites—what was it? 'subvertedBritain dotcom' or some such crap—filled with shit about how Jews were parasites and traitors and they worshipped a demon. And we believed them."

"And now?" Verity said.

He shook his head. "Now I've a couple of mates in here who are Muslims, a couple of darkies, and one who's a Jew. And they're fucking good mates. One thing about this place is you have to decide who's any fucking good based on what they do, not what some fucker says about them."

"No Eskimo friends yet, then?" Verity said.

He grinned at her. "Not yet. Though you never know."

Cecilia smiled. Evidently he fancied Verity. Not that that was a surprise.

"You know," Williams was saying, "everyone says how fucking evil we were—the Nazis, the National Front, British Nationalists, English Defence League, British Union all that—and they're right. We were. I know that. But there *were* reasons. There were hardly any jobs, factories where our dads had worked for years for a decent wage had been shut down, the government was smashing up the unions, Arab millionaires were buying up everything and everywhere you looked in London there were darkies running around in long dresses who couldn't even speak English and didn't want to. We were scared. It's the same now with a lot of those idiots who voted for Brexit. They're scared. I'm not saying that makes what we did right. It doesn't. But I tell you this—it's a sight easier to say, 'I hate Jews' or 'I hate niggers' than it is to say 'I'm scared.'"

Cecilia gazed at him and nodded slowly. She was impressed.

"I think there was another fellow with you," she said after a moment. "On the night of the fire—William Craig? Do you know anything about what happened to him?"

"Craig! *William* Craig! Always insisted on 'William'. Wouldn't answer to Bill or Billy like any normal bloke. Yes, well, William Craig pinned his ears back and fuckin' did a runner, didn't he? Never saw him again."

"So you've no idea what happened to him?"

"No. 'Course he wasn't like most of us. That little fucker had money, always posh suits, spoke proper—well, *he* wasn't scared like the rest of us were—worried about jobs or money or somewhere decent to live. For him it was all in his head. He used to go on about how us whites had beaten everyone else and taken over their countries. So that showed we was better than them and had a *right* to be in charge, and they needed to do what they was told."

"Might equals right," Verity said. "The strong do what they have power to do and the weak accept what they must."

Williams stared at her for a moment. "That's right," he said. "That's *exactly* what he told us. That's how he said it. He said it was what the ancient Greeks said."

Verity nodded. "It's what the Athenians told the Melians. It's in Thucydides' *History of the Peloponnesian War.*"

Cecilia watched this exchange fascinated. Williams appeared to be genuinely interested in what Verity was saying.

"But that don't make it right," he pointed out.

"No," Verity said. "And Thucydides knew it didn't."

"Did he? Well I can tell you William Craig didn't bother telling us about that part. He just told us we had the *right* to be in charge because we *could* be, and that meant we whites ought to stick together."

"But you don't know what happened to him?"

He shook his head.

"Even your lot couldn't find him. Some rich prick covered for him, I'll bet. One thing's for sure: for all his talk about whites sticking together, the little fucker wasn't going to stick by us when the shit hit the fan."

TWENTY

Michael Aarons' study in Saint Mary's Rectory, Exeter.
About the same time.

"Well father, you certainly seem to have gotten into a ticklish situation—and through no fault of your own, so far as I can see."

Michael was on the phone. He had just described his dilemma to his spiritual director. There was a pause, and he heard a faint tapping.

He smiled. Father Joseph was tapping his fingers on the desk, just as he always did when he was thinking hard.

"Well," his director said finally, "first of all let me be sure I've got it right—you didn't hear the poor fellow's confession, did you? This was simply a pastoral conversation?"

"Yes, father. Since he was obviously penitent, I naturally assured him that God *always* forgives sinners who are sorry for their sins and trying to amend their lives. And I was thinking that later on, when he was a bit more used to our ways, I *would* offer him the option of making a first confession. But for the moment this was just a conversation."

"Good. Apropos which conversation, however, you still

consider yourself bound by confidentiality, just as you were at the time it took place?"

"I do."

"Good. Because a man's dead, that doesn't give us the right to ignore our commitments to him. But now we've got a situation in which your silence *might* harm the living—even cause someone to lose their life?"

"And that's what worries me."

"Of course it does." A pause. "Now father, I'm sure you've wrestled in prayer over this, but even so I'm wondering—did it never occur to you God might have put you in this position precisely so you could use this information to save someone's life?"

Michael drew in his breath sharply. Such a thought had not even crossed his mind. He'd seen the thing entirely as a burden, an albatross around his neck, even a threat—but never as an opportunity.

"I must admit it didn't," he said.

"Well I don't think we should rule that possibility out. Confidentiality, like a lot of things—such as not driving your car through the traffic lights when they're red!—is an ethical norm. But it's not a moral law. And not causing harm to other people is an ethical norm too. In my experience, most times when we find ourselves in a situation where two ethical norms seem to be in conflict, it simply means God wants us to weigh the options carefully. In this case your duty not to place another life at risk must to some extent modify your duty to keep confidentiality. I'm not saying that means forget about confidentiality. You'll still want to be as discreet as you can. But we need to look for a way through."

Michael found himself nodding. Of course this was what he needed to hear. How often he'd counselled others not to confuse ethical norms with moral laws! Who was it said that most of the time we don't need to be taught something fresh but to be reminded of what we already know?

But Father Joseph hadn't finished. "How about this for a suggestion? Couldn't you maybe just *tell* your wife what are the people and places where you think she might usefully look for clues and connections to the murderer she's trying to catch? Make it clear you're not in a position to explain *why* you think what you think, but also make it clear you're pretty sure your information's good. If Cecilia is half the woman I think she is, she'll get the point. She knows your commitments. She won't ask you to explain. She'll follow up on your suggestions and find out for herself what she needs to know. Does that sound feasible?"

Michael smiled. Of course that was exactly what Cecilia would do. He should have realized that himself.

"Indeed it does. Thank you."

"I know you've only met her once," he added after a moment, "but I sometimes think you know my wife better than I do!"

There was a chuckle from the other end.

"Ah, well, father, you know what they say. Sometimes it's the onlooker sees most of the game!"

Twenty-One

The Royal Opera House, Covent Garden. Later the same day.

Tobias Heschel ("but everyone calls me 'Toby'") turned out to be a lanky, tousle haired young man in jeans, trainers and a blue tee shirt with "What fools these mortals be!" on the front. Cecilia suspected he'd bought it at the Globe, where she'd seen them on sale when she went to see *The Comedy of Errors* with papa a year or so ago. Perhaps, then, he was a fan of Shakespeare as well as the opera? As he sat down she noticed a blue yarmulke perched on his abundant curls.

Was he, then, an observant Jew?

"Yes, I'm observant," he said cheerfully, evidently reading her thought, "though I dare say not as observant as some of my orthodox family would like!"

"It must be difficult at times."

He shook his head. "As for eating—I've a simple rule. Unless I'm in a place I know is kosher, I don't eat meat at all, and no seafood unless it's got fins and scales—a proper fish! People think that sounds like a terrible burden, but it's really not. And I've yet to find myself in a situation where there was simply nothing I could eat."

What about the Sabbath?

"Everyone here's very understanding. I leave on Friday for *erev shabbat* with my family, and my colleagues know I won't be back until Saturday's over. The good news for them is, if there's a crisis that involves working on Sunday—and in this business that's quite often—then I'm first up—me and a couple of Muslims who are on the team. I think together we make it work quite well."

As for the death of Jack Hooper, Toby Heschel seemed to be as surprised and distressed in his way as the Williams brothers had been in theirs. Hearing the news, he shook his head and said softly, "*Baruch Dayan emet.*"

Blessed be the true judge.

Cecilia nodded. She'd heard Michael use the phrase more than once. Confronted with some things, there is simply nothing further to be said.

"I never knew the man," Toby said, "but I knew *of* him, and was brought up to think of him as *goy tzaddiq*—a righteous gentile—as I'd say of any gentile who protects Jews or tries to protect them. I'm sorry for this."

Nevertheless, the question had to be asked: where was Toby Heschel on the evening when Jack Hooper was murdered?

He considered for a moment, and then chuckled softly. *That* was the day there'd been a problem about one of the sets for the new show. He'd been working with the rest of the artistic direction team from three in the afternoon until well past one in the morning—"we all had bleeding eyes!" And he could call a dozen witnesses to tell the tale, as Cecilia and Verity were soon able to verify. In other words, and as Verity put it when they were leaving the building, either the entire production staff of the Royal Opera House was conspiring to lie about it, or Toby Heschel had an alibi.

TWENTY-TWO

Near the Royal Opera House, twenty minutes or so later

Their interviews complete, Cecilia led the way along Bow Street to Wellington Street, past the neo-classical façade of the Lyceum (all cream and gold and plastered with notices about *The Lion King*) and so to *The Wellington* next door: a Victorian pub named of course for the iron duke, whose portrait—looking somewhat nervously at traffic in the Strand—loomed over the main entrance. It had been one of her regular haunts during her years as a PC with the Met, and didn't seem to have changed at all, so that as she entered the crowded bar and glanced down its length she was almost surprised there was no one she knew.

"My shout," she said as they drew near the bar. "I recommend the chicken and chorizo pie, if they're still doing it."

"Right," Verity said. "And a half of whatever is their best bitter, please."

They *were* still doing it, and the barman at least she knew.

"PC Cavaliere, as I live and breathe!" he said, and then, reaching toward a bottle of Sauvignon Blanc, "Your usual?"

She laughed.

"Thanks Bill. It's good to see you—and good to know some

things don't change. Yes, I'll have my usual, please, and a half of best for my friend DI Jones. We'll both have the chicken and chorizo, if we're not too late. DI Jones, this is Bill Stevens, who keeps this place going."

"Hello," Verity said.

"Detective Inspector Jones!" he said, eyeing Verity appreciatively, "welcome to *The Wellington*. And a half of best coming up."

"And you," he said, turning his attention back to Cecilia as he finished drawing Verity's half pint, "I bet you aren't *PC* Cavaliere any more."

"She's Detective Superintendent Cavaliere," Verity said.

He whistled. "I suppose then you must be brilliant at thwarting crime."

"Oh, absolutely!" Cecilia said. "That's definitely me. Crime no sooner seen than *thwarted!*"

He chuckled.

"Well there you are. Some things *do* change, and even for the better. Two chicken chorizos. Where are you going to sit?"

Some time later, when they were settled with food and drink, Verity harked back to their morning interviews.

"I really don't think any of them had anything to do with it," she said. "I thought they were all telling the truth. They didn't even know Jack Hooper was dead until we told them."

Cecilia nodded. "Yes," she said slowly. "I think I agree with you."

The Williams brothers and Tobias Heschel had all, in their different ways, been good witnesses. They'd shown no significant confusion, nor had they evaded any question put to them. Nor had they shown any of those tiny physical signs of lying—momentary telltale reactions—that experience had taught her she had something of an instinct for spotting. And they all, of course, had significant alibis.

Verity gazed thoughtfully into her beer.

"Which means," she said at last, "that so far we're doing much better at eliminating potential suspects than we are at spotting them."

Cecilia laughed.

"Fear not!" she said. "We still have the mysterious William Craig, who was evidently a nasty bit of work, and clever enough to disappear even though everyone including us was looking for him."

"That's true," Verity said. "The only problem with that being the minor inconvenience that no one seems to have the slightest idea where he is or if he's alive or dead!"

TWENTY-THREE

St Mary's Rectory, that evening.

It was a time of day that Michael always enjoyed. The supper things were cleared away, dogs and cats had been treated as befitted them, and the children were asleep. He and Cecilia were curled up in a friendly bundle on the sofa.

She'd told him the story of her day, about visiting Belmarsh Prison and the Royal Opera house, at rather more length about her visit to the Wellington and meeting her old friend Bill Stevens the barman, and finally about her and Verity's mounting frustration at the fact that they seemed to be doing so much better at eliminating suspects in their murder investigation than at finding them.

When she'd finished he said, "About this case, I do have a couple of suggestions."

"You do?"

"The thing is, I really can't talk about why I'm making them. But I can assure you I've good reason to think they really might be worth following up."

She raised an eyebrow and gazed at him for a moment.

Then, slowly, she nodded. She'd got it—just as Father Joseph said she would.

"All right," she said quietly. "Tell me what you can."

"First of all," he said, "I think you need to be looking for someone called William Craig, a nasty piece of work, a kind of fascist intellectual, if there is such a thing."

Cecilia smiled.

"That," she said, "confirms directly what one of the prisoners at Belmarsh told me today. He hadn't much time for him either. All right, William Craig ought to be looked at. Duly noted. The only problem being what Verity calls a 'minor inconvenience'—that we haven't a clue where to start or even if he's still alive."

"Well there's more—and this may help with that. You might want to look at any connection William Craig may have to the security services."

"The security services?"

"Yes."

Cecilia raised an eyebrow.

"*That*," she said, "is a completely new idea to me."

He watched as she considered.

"But," she said slowly, "now that I come to think about it, it might fit with something Adriana Martínez told us. She said the last time Jack Hooper went up to London, he told her he'd seen someone in the street near Thames House—someone he hadn't seen for years and didn't *want* to see again. Those were more or less her exact words. And Thames House is the headquarters of MI5. So was it William Craig he saw?" She paused again, considering her own question. "It might have been. Or of course it might not. All right. Possible connection to the security services, duly noted."

"As for the other thing," Michael said, "I ought to say that even my informant wasn't at all sure what it meant, or whether it was anything significant, or whether there was anything in it at all."

The fact was, it was something Jack Hooper had heard in a pub some years ago from one of his racist friends when the friend was drunk. And it had been little enough—a mere hint.

"It's about the old memorial at the edge of the Winterbourne Woods—or rather near it. There might be something buried there, something hidden. Of course it may be nothing at all, or something long gone—but it could be worth a look."

He stopped.

"I suppose you've nothing more precise than 'near'?" she said.

He shook his head. "Sorry."

"Okay." Cecilia met his eye and gave a teasing little smile. "And that's it? That's what you've got?"

"That's it, I'm afraid. If I think of something else I can tell you, of course I will."

"Fair enough." She paused. "To be honest, I was starting to feel we were running out of options. You may have just opened up a whole new area of investigation. In fact, several new areas! Thank you."

Michael grinned at her. "Thank *you*," he said.

The ache of anxiety that had been in his gut virtually every moment since he learned of Jack Hooper's death was suddenly gone.

And Cecilia had, of course, reacted precisely as Father Joseph— despite having met her only once, and briefly at that—had known she would.

He was a lucky man.

Twenty-Four

"A possible connection to the security services?"

Glyn Davies appeared to be as surprised by the suggestion as Cecilia had been.

"And you had this from an informant you trust?"

"I did, sir. He's never given me information that didn't turn out to be correct."

Davies nodded, and pursed his lips.

"Then I take it seriously. Though we'll need to tread carefully on how we follow up on it."

She took his point. Relationships between the police and the security services, both of them concerned for the peace and safety of the realm, ought to have been harmonious and sometimes even were: but not always, and especially not recently. Arguments about jurisdiction and boundaries, assertions of police blundering into delicate situations and ruining undercover operations and a dozen other reasons for dispute could cause ruffled feathers or worse. Tact would be needed.

"If only Ian Salmon were still alive, I'd go to him," Glyn Davies said.

Again Cecilia took his point. This was just one more way in which the commander's death had left a gap that was not easily filled.

"However," Glyn Davies continued, "I think I know one other person I can consult. The Director General. He was my CO at one point."

"Ashley-Cooper? I thought he didn't like us much."

"Henry Saint John Ashley-Cooper *doesn't* like us much. In fact, I'd say he doesn't like us at all! But he's only the *Acting* Director General. I mean the real Director General. I mean Bernard Hough. We served together in the army. To be precise, for the best part of a year he was my C.O. Anyway, he trusts me and I trust him. If I ask to see him he'll see me."

Sir Bernard Hough, VC—of course she knew of him, although she hadn't realized Glyn Davies' previous connection with him. And she knew that he'd been given leave because of illness.

"I thought Sir Bernard was a sick man. Isn't he still on leave?"

"He is. But that doesn't mean he's lost his wits. And he *is* still the director of MI5. If a fanatic bigot such as Craig seems to have been was somehow involved in the security services, Bernard would want to know about it." He sighed. "To be frank, I'm *not* happy about troubling him while he's ill, but he's the only person who can be some use that I know I can trust. If I go blundering in and talk to anyone else—even Ashley-Cooper, whom I really *don't* know—it's my view I risk doing precisely what they're always accusing us of doing: giving a heads-up to the very people we might be out to catch."

He paused again, and then said, "Well, let me worry about that. For the moment Cecilia, I suggest this stays within this room until we know what Bernard has to say. Now, what on earth are we going to do about your informant's other suggestion—the Winterbourne Woods thing?"

"He seemed to think it might be important."

"Maybe it is," he said. "The problem is it's so vague. 'Near the old memorial' could mean almost anything: five metres away or fifty in any direction—and much of it completely overgrown, as I recall. To search an area that big in that terrain and do it properly will need quite a few officers, and at the moment we simply haven't got them. I know it's frustrating, but I honestly don't see how we can get to it for the next week or so. You know how stretched we are."

Again Cecilia nodded.

"As far as that's concerned," she said, "my impression is, if there's anything in it, whatever it is has been there for a decade or so, so I suppose a bit of delay won't make *too* much difference."

Glyn Davies nodded grimly. "It won't have to."

"Meanwhile," she said, "there's mass of other stuff—a lot of new paperwork—that I ought to get onto."

Odd, she thought, how we still call it that, even though I'll be doing virtually all of it on the computer.

"I expect there is," said Davies. "All right, then. You crack on with that."

TWENTY-FIVE

Exmouth Seafront, at about the same time.

PCs George Task and Charlie Simmons, nearing the end of their period of duty, drove slowly along the Queens Drive at Exmouth. They were just passing Maer Lane when Charlie noticed something coloured down on the beach. It was early morning and the two-mile long stretch of sand was still deserted, so the something stood out rather clearly.

"What do you think that is?" he said.

George pulled the car over and parked in the space by the lifeboat station. The two officers got out, walked to the edge of the tarmac, and peered down. They'd already completed a couple of hours extra duty to cover a gap in the schedule—cost cutting and a lack of officers being, as so often these days, the cause—and both were tired. It would be idle to pretend that either of them was not tempted to mutter, "Just some moron leaving his rubbish about!" and get back into the car and drive on, but then—

"Bugger it! We'd better take a look," George said, and Charlie nodded reluctantly.

So they walked down the lifeboat slipway, then out along the sand and across to whatever-it-was: which turned out to be a pile of clothes, neatly folded, with a pair of brown loafers beside it. Charlie's eye had been caught by a brightly coloured tie laid out on top. He was quite surprised that it hadn't blown away.

"Some college boy pissed out of his mind decided on a midnight swim and then forgot where he left his stuff?" Charlie speculated.

George considered for a minute and then shook his head. "I doubt a plastered idiot deciding on a swim would have left his stuff like this. It'd be all higgledy-piggledy in a heap."

Charlie nodded. "That's true."

George knelt down and felt carefully among the clothes, disturbing them as little as possible.

"This is good quality stuff," he muttered as he did so.

"But so far as I can see," he added a few seconds later, "there's no ID. If he had a wallet or anything it's gone."

"Maybe it's been nicked."

"Maybe it has."

George got to his feet, brushing loose sand from his trousers as he did so. The two officers stood for a moment looking around the beach. Apart from themselves it was deserted: nothing but waves lapping gently on sand and a few seagulls wheeling and dipping above them.

"This could be serious," George said finally. "I'm calling it in."

Shortage of officers meant that the Exmouth Station wouldn't be open for another hour. So George had to put his call through to Heavitree, which was irritating because it surely meant the response time would be slower.

At Heavitree, however, Sergeant Stillwell on the desk also thought it might be serious and passed it straight on to Cecilia, who was by now, as she'd promised Glyn Davies, back in her office and up to her eyes in so-called paperwork.

But she, too, thought it might be serious.

"It sounds to me as though they need a dog," she said, and called for one.

Tempted to abandon the office and the paperwork for a visit to the beach, she resisted temptation and instead sent Tom Wilkins to see what was going on.

TWENTY-SIX

The beach at Exmouth, about forty minutes later.

Tom wasted no time. He set off at once and met with no serious delays as he drove the eleven or so miles from Exeter to Exmouth beach. Even so, by the time he arrived, in addition to Charlie and George there were two more uniformed officers on the scene who, he gathered, had been there for about twenty minutes.

Minutes later the dog handler arrived. This was PC Brenda Cosgrove, whom Tom knew and had even dated a couple of times before she got engaged. PC Brenda was accompanied by Snipe the sniffer, a cheerful springer spaniel whose tail never seemed to stop wagging.

Handler and dog wasted no time. Indeed, the pair of them had not been on the scene for much more than five minutes before Snipe, having looked at the heap of clothes and sniffed them, had found their owner in a shallow grave behind the dunes some fifty or so metres away.

"We've got something," PC Brenda shouted.

By the time Tom got to her and a triumphant Snipe, who now stood back wagging his tail more energetically than ever, she was gently scraping back the sand. Within seconds she had exposed a face: eyes staring, young, clean-shaven, and very dead.

Tom shook his head.

"Not much more than a kid," he said. "This is bloody awful."

Brenda nodded, then turned to give Snipe a well-earned biscuit and a pat on the head, as from one professional crime-fighter to another.

"And we've no ID yet," he said.

But then an unexpected voice came from behind him.

"I think I know who he is."

Tom looked round and recognized the uniformed officer who had spoken. It was PC Annwn Merchant.

"You know him?" he said.

"He's one of the blokes who came up to us the other night when Sam Devlin and I were in Topsham watching the *Falcon*. They were both drunk, or seemed to be. Harmless, but drunk. Leastways, that's what we thought. Anyway, he said his mother was a Mrs Cornellissen in Topsham. Mrs Letitia Cornellissen of Ambrose House. Very keen he was for us to know that, now I come to think about it."

TWENTY-SEVEN

Topsham. The same morning, about an hour later

Tom took PC Annwn with him to see Mrs Cornellissen in Topsham. Ambrose House, it turned out, was a handsome seventeenth century building just off Ferry Road. Mrs Cornellissen herself was a tall, striking woman, beautifully dressed. She looked somewhat surprised when he introduced himself and PC Merchant, but stood aside without comment when he asked, "May we come in?" and showed them into a small, elegantly furnished parlour. She turned and looked at the two officers expectantly.

He went straight to the point.

"Mrs Cornellissen," he said, "I believe you have a son."

"I do. Robert Cornellissen. Why?"

"Do you know where your son is, ma'am?"

"He's in the City. He works for Van Huyten's, the merchant bankers. He has a flat in town. He's only at home at weekends."

"And when did you last speak to him?"

"Yesterday morning. Why?"

"And he's at work now?"

"Of course."

"Would it be possible for you to call him?"

"I could, but he won't like it."

"It might be important."

She shrugged, picked up a telephone, and punched in a number.

"Good morning, this is Mrs Cornellissen. Could you put me through for a moment to my son Robert? In Acquisitions."

The voice on the other end of the phone said something that Tom could not make out.

Mrs Cornellissen looked surprised.

"Oh. I see."

There was something more from the phone.

"I see. Well thank you. I must have misunderstood something he said."

She replaced the handset and looked at Tom. "They say he isn't at work this morning and wasn't there yesterday afternoon either. He went out at lunchtime and no one has seen him since. This is not like him. I'll try his mobile."

Tom nodded in acquiescence and they waited while she did so. Even from where he stood he could hear the response, blank and impersonal: "The mobile number you have called is not available. Please try again later."

Mrs Cornellissen frowned and looked at the officers and shook her head. "I confess I'm concerned. As I say, this isn't like him."

Tom sighed. The truth was, despite what Annwn Merchant said on the beach, he'd been hoping against hope that her identification would be wrong and Mrs Cornellissen's son would turn out to be at his desk in the bank. That hope had died, and what must now be done was a part of his job that he hated more than anything—

But then as he was about to speak, Annwn held up her hand to stop him. He was surprised, but waited. She pointed to a silver-framed photograph that stood on the table beside the telephone.

"Excuse me, ma'am," she said, "but is that you with your son Robert?"

"It is."

"May I?"

"If you wish."

Annwn picked it up. "And it's a good likeness?" she said.

"I think so."

"And you have no other son?"

"No, officer." Mrs Cornellissen was still polite, but there was a trace of irritation in her tone, which Tom was beginning to share. What the hell was PC Merchant up to?

"Thank you, ma'am." Annwn turned and passed the photograph to Tom.

He found himself looking at a picture of Mrs Cornellissen standing in a garden. With her, his arm round her shoulders, was a tall young man—taller even than she—with long blonde hair and a short blonde beard.

He gave a slight, involuntary gasp. Thank God Annwn had stopped him in time!

Whoever was the young man whose body they'd found on the beach, he wasn't the young man in this photograph.

"Well, officer?" Mrs Cornellissen was finally losing patience. He could understand why.

He shook his head.

"I apologize, ma'am. The fact is, we found someone—a body—down on the beach—and we had reason at first to think it might be your son. I'm happy to say it very clearly isn't. That said—your son does appear to be missing. We need to look into that."

"I'd be grateful if you would." She hesitated. "Doesn't he have to be gone forty-eight hours or something before it counts? Before you can do anything?"

Tom shook his head. It was strange how often people thought that. He'd met a woman a few weeks back who believed you had to be gone a week before the police would act! It was of course nonsense. The fact was, if someone's whereabouts were unknown and there was reason for concern, the police would regard them as "missing" even if they'd only been gone for a couple of hours.

"No, ma'am," he said, "he doesn't have to have been gone that long. We'll see to it that the Metropolitan police are notified. They'll look into it."

TWENTY-EIGHT

An MI5 safe house, somewhere in Dorset.
The same morning

The chief superintendent's request for an interview with Sir Bernard Hough had been granted promptly, and then, on a "need-to-know" basis, he'd been collected and driven in a closed car to the safe house unit where his former C.O. was recovering from his operation.

Seated in an armchair in a sunny, pleasantly furnished lounge, with a pile of official looking papers on a table beside him, Sir Bernard looked paler and more fragile than when Glyn Davies had last seen him. But still he seemed bright and alert as he quickly laid aside the papers he was reading, rose from his chair and greeted with evident pleasure his old friend and comrade in arms. An army medic brought them tea and biscuits, and they chatted for a while—first, about Sir Bernard's health, which was, so his doctors assured him, very much on the mend.

"They reckon I can be back in full harness any day now," he said. "And between me and you I can't wait! Of course everyone here is very kind. Indeed, at times they're so kind they drive me dotty! It'll be a real pleasure to be back in Thames House at my desk amid all the angst and good old-fashioned intersectional bitching and complaining."

Glyn chuckled even as Sir Bernard shook his head.

"For remarks like that I, of course, deserve to be castigated as an ungrateful bastard! The people here are wonderful at what they do and I've every reason to be damned grateful."

"But you're still looking forward to getting back to work."

"Exactly."

For a few minutes the two talked about army days and news of old friends. It was Sir Bernard who finally said, "Glyn, pleasant though this is, you surely didn't travel all the way here to listen to my complaints and share war stories. There was something you needed to talk about, I think?"

Glyn Davies nodded. "Yes, sir. There was."

He laid out briefly all that had taken place over the last few days—the murder of Jack Hooper, the suggestion from a generally reliable informant that a right wing extremist called William Craig was somehow involved in that murder, and the further suggestion that said William Craig had some connection to the security services.

"Detective Superintendent Cavaliere trusts this informant, who has always given her good information before. And I trust Cavaliere's judgment. So I come to you."

Sir Bernard listened attentively, fingers together. He took no notes, but if he were the man Glyn Davies remembered, he didn't need to. His ability to recall what had been said in a conversation had always been frightening—virtually one hundred per cent.

"I recall our friend Ian Salmon formed a very high opinion of Cavaliere," he said.

He sat in silence for a further minute.

"Glyn," he said finally, "can you give me a day to think about this and make some enquiries? Are you going back to Exeter today?"

"I really need to, sir."

"Do you have a number that I can call discreetly? A *secure* number?"

Glyn Davies took a card out his wallet, wrote on it, and handed it to Sir Bernard, who looked at it and nodded.

"Excellent. God willing, I shall call you on this number at ten o'clock tomorrow morning. I should by then know whether I can help you."

TWENTY-NINE

Heavitree Police Station. Later the same morning.

Some things were quickly dealt with. PC Sam Devlin, when found and asked to view the body from the beach, promptly made the same identification as his colleague.

When asked whether the young man in Mrs Cornellisssen's photograph might perhaps be the *taller* of the two who had approached them while they were watching over the *Falcon*, both officers were equally sure that he was not.

"The other chap who came up to us was tall all right," Sam said, "but not like this chap. Our chap was dark and skinny."

Annwn agreed. "This Cornellissen bloke is big built and blonde—a Viking hero type. I could definitely fancy him."

The cause of death was also straightforward.

"Not much problem there," Tom Foss said to Cecilia later that morning. She was sitting in her office with Verity, listening to the speakerphone. "Two gun shots to the chest at almost point-blank range. The bullets took him in the heart. Death would have been more or less instantaneous."

"And he was shot like that after he'd taken his clothes off?" Verity said.

"Apparently. Except for his underpants. But before you draw too many conclusions about that, talk to Sergeant Coulter about the bullet and the weapon. There could be another reason other than the killer being a complete weirdo."

"Will do, Tom."

Sergeant Bob Coulter was an ex-army man who led the armed response unit when needed and who knew (as he sometimes put it himself) "more than he really wanted to" about guns. He was also engaged to PC Brenda Cosgrove. The couple were receiving pre-marriage counselling from Michael.

As it happened Bob Coulter was in the building and available. He arrived at Cecilia's office within minutes.

"Doctor Foss thought you might have something to tell us about why our victim was undressed before he was shot," Verity said. "Other, of course, than our killer having a taste for such things."

"Well there might be a practical reason," he said. "The bullets that killed the young man were 2.7 mm Kolibris."

"You've already lost me, sergeant," Cecilia said. "Is that good?"

He grinned. "I'm not sure whether it's good or not, ma'am. But it's interesting."

She and Verity looked at each other and then back at him.

"'Kolibri' is German for hummingbird," he said, "and the 2.7 mm Kolibri is the tiniest centrefire cartridge ever made."

"Centrefire cartridge?" Cecilia asked.

"Cartridges designed for guns that have the primer in the centre of the base."

"Aren't all modern guns like that?" Verity said.

"There's still a place for rimfire, ma'am. If you want something low calibre, say maybe a .22 rifle to shoot rats. But you're essentially right. As far as serious weapons are concerned, rimfire is old tech. Anyway, as I say, this particular bullet is unique. It's the tiniest of its kind ever made. It was meant to be fired from a 2.7 mm semi-automatic pistol that an Austrian watchmaker designed in around

1910. There was something of a craze for tiny guns in the early nineteen hundreds, and this played right into it: it was less than eight centimetres long and weighed about two hundred grams. But the other thing you need to know about it is that only about a thousand of them were ever made, *so it's now very rare*. Examples of the breed in good working condition can fetch thousands at auction."

"And you can still get ammunition for it?"

"If you know where to look. It'd probably cost you about fifty pounds a cartridge, though."

"So if it's that rare and expensive, it's almost as if the killer who used it left a calling card with his name on it, isn't it?" Cecilia said. "We might be able to trace who bought or owns such a gun? Or who bought such ammunition?"

Bob Coulter nodded. "Yes, ma'am."

"Or *her* name," Verity said. "This sounds like the kind of gun a girl could slip into her purse along with her lipstick and compact. The ultimate accessory!"

"And how," Cecilia said, returning to the original point, "would all this be a possible reason for the victim being undressed before he was shot?"

He chuckled. "Oh, yes—I was forgetting about that! Well the fact is, because it's so small, a shot from a 2.7 mm Kolibri doesn't generate a huge amount of energy, which means that it *could* merely bounce off thick clothing. So if you want to be sure you get your man, it's as well to strip him."

"Or else use a bigger gun," Cecilia said.

Again he chuckled. "Yes, ma'am."

THIRTY

A t the full team meeting that afternoon, they went over all that
they had learned. At the end of which recital and discus-
sion Cecilia said, "So, the sum of it all is that instead of one corpse
we now have two, and we have killer with a taste for tiny antique
guns. Indirectly we have also a missing person—though since he
lives in London and was last seen there, at the moment that's a case
for the Met."

"But they're all somehow linked," Verity said.

"I suppose we're sure of that?"

Verity shook her head. "I'm not saying we know *how* they're
linked or why. But there's no getting round the fact that victim
number two came to the *exact* place where victim number one
had been murdered and where the killer was still hanging out,
though we didn't know that at the time. And then victim number
two loudly though falsely proclaimed that he was the son of Mrs
Cornellissen, which is to say, *he loudly identified himself with our now
missing person*. Those are *links*, whatever they mean."

There seemed to be no arguing with that.

Cecilia looked at Joseph. "And still there's nothing on William Craig," she said.

"Nothing more so far. But I haven't given up."

Cecilia swallowed a smile. "Of course you haven't."

The truth was, Joseph was more frustrated in the matter of William Craig than he cared to admit. Of course he liked to joke about being an obsessive compulsive with access to the Internet. But he was good at what he did and he knew it. And he'd been able to provide his colleagues with information they needed to move forward on a case on more occasions than either they or he could remember.

But not this time.

He'd asked for and been granted access to the old Met file on the original search for Craig, and its content pointed to the same frustration among his colleagues seventeen or so years ago as now. William Craig, it seemed, really had vanished. There were those last sightings in France and then nothing. Sometimes he was tempted to think his quarry must be dead. But in truth he doubted it. If Craig had died there would have been a hint of it somewhere. Instead, his gut told him the man was still out there. One just needed to find him. But to do that he needed a hook, a marker, something to go on.

And as yet he had nothing.

THIRTY-ONE

Heavitree Police Station, Cecilia's office.
About an hour later.

The day did, however, have one more revelation in store for Cecilia and her colleagues.

It came at just on five o'clock. She'd brought the team meeting to a close. People were gathering their stuff together and preparing to leave when the phone on her desk buzzed.

"Hang on," she said peering at it. "It's Tom Foss. He may have something for us."

She picked up. "Yes, Tom?"

"I've got something new about our corpse on the beach," he said.

She switched to speakerphone so that they could all hear.

"Go on," she said. "We're all listening."

"I just got back the DNA report," he said. "I had the lab rush it."

Like those annoying television presenters whose job is to open the sealed envelope and tell the world who has won whatever it is, Tom Foss enjoyed his dramatic pauses. So now he allowed several irritating seconds to pass before he said, "It's fifty-three per cent identical to the DNA we obtained from Hooper's boat—the DNA of the man who killed Hooper, Marcel Gagnon."

He hesitated, this time only slightly, before adding, "You know what that means, don't you?"

Cecilia looked at her colleagues. Verity blew out her cheeks. Joseph and Headley gave half smiles. Tom raised both eyebrows. Actually they *did* know what it meant. As luck would have it, some months ago they'd all attended a seminar together on this very subject.

"It means," Cecilia said, "that our murder victim on the beach was either Marcel Gagnon's brother or else his son."

Given the evident youth of the corpse on the beach, she reckoned she might reasonably rule out the possibility that he was Gagnon's father.

"That's right," Tom Foss said, sounding only minimally deflated. "It does. Actually, his DNA's on the Interpol database, too, as are his fingerprints. It's the fellow I mentioned to you before: Marcel Gagnon's younger brother, Armand Gagnon. The database has him down as small time criminal and blackmailer."

THIRTY-TWO

London: Thames House, Millbank.
9.40 a.m. Wednesday, 12th September.

The man in charge was in his office, ensconced as he liked to be behind a vast nineteenth century mahogany desk that dominated the room.

Everything was as it should be.

But then, as he surveyed his surroundings, he frowned. Everything was *not* as it should be! He tutted irritably, rose to his feet, walked round the desk and crossed to the wall facing it. There, on the wall to the right of the door, he minutely adjusted the position of a framed copy of Vincent Brooks' 1851 colour lithograph *The Fire Proof Sugar Refinery Erected for Messrs Charles & John Frederick Bowman* so that it aligned more perfectly with Thomas Shotter Boys' 1843 tinted lithograph *The Bank, looking towards Mansion House* on its left. He went back to his desk, again seated himself, and observed the results of his labours.

After a careful moment, he nodded. The positioning was now satisfactory.

There was a discreet knock.

"Come!"

His secretary entered as if on tiptoe and laid an envelope on his desk with a whispered, "This just came for you, sir."

He nodded, but otherwise did not move until she had gone. He then picked it up, slit it open neatly with the gold and platinum letter opener that normally sat six inches away from the base of his desk light and at right angles to it, replaced the letter opener in the position from which he had taken it, extracted a sheet of paper from the envelope, and dropped the envelope itself into an otherwise empty waste paper basket on his left.

He unfolded the paper, glanced at it, and nodded.

Good. The little attempt at blackmail had, to be sure, been an unpleasant surprise, and he had felt obliged to deal with it himself, which was always slightly dangerous. But then, the look of amazement on the young man's face when he died had surely made it worth it.

So much for the negatives! On the positive side, the American document had arrived and already been distributed. Right thinking colleagues across the Atlantic had seen to that, and as a result of their action, his own group were almost ready for their next move. The memorandum he had just received confirmed that at least one person in a high place would, at the right moment, be willing to support them.

He refolded the sheet of paper and placed it in a drawer to his right, which he was careful to lock.

THIRTY-THREE

*Exeter: Heavitree Police Station, the Chief Superintendent's office.
A few minutes later.*

True to his word, Sir Bernard called Glyn Davies on his secure line at ten o'clock precisely on the morning following their conversation.

"Are you alone?"

"Yes."

"Good."

He came straight to the point.

"Well the first thing I have to say is that I've failed. I can find no evidence of your William Craig ever having had anything to do with the security services—and I had some people I trust go back twenty years to be sure I covered the ground. If he *is* in here, he is very well covered indeed. Which I dare say is disappointing for you. I'm sorry."

"One can only look, sir."

"That's true. But still it's disappointing." He paused, and then said, "I can, however, offer you one straw at which you may wish to clutch. I've had quite a recent memorandum—last week, to be exact, from the Foreign Office, from the PUS himself, in fact—"

"The PUS?"

"The Permanent Under Secretary. He's concerned that there *may* be an extremist right wing rogue element operating in the security services. There have been rumours, and he wants me to look into them. Now, let me say at once, even if he's right, I've absolutely no idea whether this has any connection at all to your William Craig or to the murder your people are investigating. It may be completely *un*related. The one common thread I can see between our problem and yours, and I admit it's a pretty thin one, is right wing extremism."

"We can look into it and see what comes of it."

"Agreed," Sir Bernard said. "My problem—and I've been cogitating on this since I got the under secretary's memo—my problem is, *how* shall we look into it? Socrates seems to have thought self-examination good for the soul, and perhaps that's true of individuals, though I doubt he was right that sin is merely ignorance. When an *organization* tries to examine itself, however, it's not so straightforward. There's always the chance—even a likelihood—of alerting the very persons responsible for whatever may be wrong and giving them the chance to cover their tracks. That's my concern."

That was, of course, the problem with moles and traitors. Once you thought you had one, everybody was under suspicion.

"But," Sir Bernard said, "an investigation from *outside*, if discreet, might be another matter. Do you still have the same team working with you that Ian admired so much?"

"I do, sir."

"He talked to me several times about a civilian—Joseph Stirrup, I think, is his name—a young man."

"That's right."

"According to Ian, the young man is something of a computer genius. Would you concur?"

"I would, sir."

"But also completely trustworthy?"

"Absolutely."

"Good. Well, let me fill you in with some background to the permanent under secretary's problem, and you'll see why I'm asking about your computer man. He thinks that our problem if we have one must be something to do with hacking. Of course by now it's common knowledge the Russians interfered with the last American presidential election, and the same is true of the Brexit referendum. Our own and the American intelligence agencies have uncovered overwhelming evidence of that. And of course as regards Brexit, there are obviously those in Russia who are delighted to see a weakened and divided Europe."

"You think that interference actually changed the result of the referendum?" Glyn asked. "I understood there was no clear evidence it had."

"How the blazes would one collect such evidence? And who's tried to? There surely *was* interference, and personally I find it hard to believe it had no effect at all."

"Point taken."

"When you add to that pretty clear evidence that during the referendum campaign the 'Leave' side not only lied repeatedly but also broke EU spending rules—between you and me there's mounting evidence that millions went into their campaign from impermissible sources—quite why the result hasn't been declared invalid is a mystery to me. My suspicion is it's finally down to politicians who care more for their careers than for the country being reluctant to admit they allowed what the PM calls 'the largest democratic vote in our history' to have been screwed up under their noses. That said, as the date for our leaving the European Union approaches, I suspect those same politicians are going to find it more and more difficult to produce any kind of coherent approach to it. Parliament will be paralysed. And that will be because those MPs who have any brains or sense of history at all will know in their hearts that Brexit is lunacy."

Glyn Davies, no fan of Brexit himself, was surprised. He had not heard his former CO express himself so forcibly before.

"You don't see *any* advantages in our leaving the union?" he said.

"I do not. 'Splendid isolation' was a bad idea when we were at the height of our imperial power. Now it's ten times worse. In my view never before in our history have we embarked on a project so perfectly calculated to break up the United Kingdom, at the same time rendering us economically and spiritually poorer, less able to control our own destiny and more vulnerable to those who wish us harm."

He paused.

"Still," he said, "regrettable though those things are, they're not my immediate concern. My immediate concern is that some of our own people in the security services may now be involved in planning something even bigger. It's good we blew the cover on Cambridge Analytica, but the PUS thinks that Cambridge Analytica may have been no more than the tip of an iceberg. And I must admit he's convinced me."

"That's disturbing."

"To put it mildly! But here's the rub. For all our suspicions, we don't know what's actually going on or who's directly involved. There *is* a particular section in Thames House I'm concerned about, but that's as far as I can go. And that's where I think your young man may be able to help."

Glyn Davies nodded—and then realized that Sir Bernard could not see him and said, "Yes, sir."

"You, of course, will by now have noticed what is happening. You came to me asking for help, which I have singularly failed to provide. I am now compounding that failure by asking *you* to help me!"

Glyn Davies chuckled.

"That's all right sir. And as you said yourself, this *might* have a connection to our murder or even to our elusive Mr Craig. We shan't know until we look."

If his years in the force had taught him anything, it was surely that you shouldn't take anything for granted. But Sir Bernard had not finished.

"Well then, what I'm going to do now is to give you some codes and passwords. They should get your young man past whatever firewalls the department has put up, and into the records of the particular section I'm concerned about. After that I rather suspect he's good enough to explore on his own. I'd like to know what he finds."

Glyn Davies smiled. "As our friend Ian would have put it, that sounds like a plan, sir."

Sir Bernard chuckled. "Yes, I believe that's exactly how he would have put it. Now, Glyn, you'll need to write these down and I need to make sure I get them right. We don't want to be supplying our genius with duff information."

THIRTY-FOUR

Heavitree Police Station. About an hour later.

W orking on the general basis of "need to know", Glyn Davies passed the full details of Sir Bernard's highly confidential information only on to Joseph. But of course he made sure that Cecilia was informed of the overall strategy being followed, and she smiled when she saw the gleam in Joseph's eye.

"This looks interesting," he said as he went off to what he sometimes referred to as "the boffins' underground kingdom".

"And who knows," he added over his shoulder, "it might even have something to do with our murder."

Or of course it might not.

Cecilia sighed.

The truth was, for all the information they'd gathered so far and the leads they'd followed, they'd made little or no progress. None of it seemed to make any sense.

She thought of Jack Hooper's battered and broken head, of the bullet holes in the young man on the beach. Last night she and papa had watched *Julius Caesar* in black and white on an old DVD. Could it happen that Joseph and his computer would be instruments of justice for those wounds? Would they indeed,

in these confines with a monarch's voice
Cry "Havoc!" and let slip the dogs of war,
That this foul deed shall smell above the earth
With carrion men, groaning for burial?

THIRTY-FIVE

Near Exeter: close to the Winterbourne Memorial.
The following morning.

Glyn Davies had not forgotten his promise to act when he could on the other part of Cecilia's information—the mysterious "something" that might be somewhere near the Winterbourne Memorial. Considerably sooner, in fact, than he had promised, a team was assembled under the general direction of Sergeant Coulter to begin examination of the ground round the Winterbourne Memorial, a weather-worn and battered obelisk erected at some time in the early nineteenth century to honour and memorialize a local worthy. Alas, the local worthy's name, beaten by wind and rain, had over the following century or so disappeared from the stone that was meant to honour it, and no one Cecilia now asked could tell her who it was. Even Bob Coulter, often a mine of surprising information, had no idea. Dutifully— she was, after all, the daughter of a professor of classics—she remembered her Latin: *sic transit gloria mundi*. At the same time she resolved to ask Google when she had time.

Since the information that Michael had been able to give her—"near the Winterbourne Memorial"—was so vague, she'd determined the searchers should proceed metre by metre out from the obelisk by widening circles, beginning with an area ten metres across, and then increasing by five metre jumps until (it was to be hoped) they found something.

It was a bright day, with a slight breeze alleviating the heat. There were wildflowers and even, surprisingly, a rabbit, who gazed at the team of officers with apparent amazement and incredulity before hopping away into long grass. The scene seemed fitter for a family picnic than searching for traces of an unknown crime. Nevertheless—

"Anything strange or suspicious," she told them, "let me or Sergeant Coulter know. The fact is, we're not sure what we're looking for, but we have information from a generally reliable source that suggests we'll recognize it when we find it."

Which hardly amounted to satisfactory directions for a search, as dubious expressions and odd looks among the assembled officers made clear. It was, nonetheless, all she had.

She shrugged, wordlessly acknowledging their—and her own—uncertainty.

"Do your best," she said. "Let's see what turns up."

THIRTY-SIX

In the middle of the afternoon Joseph called the Chief Super-intendent's office and asked if he might make a preliminary report on "the materials he gave me yesterday."

Glyn Davies was busy dealing with cruelty-to-animals statistics, of which there appeared to be a depressing spike in Devon and Cornwall, and, more positively, with statistics supporting a proposal that the police be enabled to recommend mental health care for individuals who had committed no crime but appeared likely to need help—which seemed to him like a useful idea. He whistled with surprise when his secretary brought Joseph's request, but was not especially unhappy at the prospect of laying aside the statistics.

He glanced around his office. Walls have ears.

"Tell him to meet me in the car park in ten minutes," he said.

When they met, Joseph looked tired but also somewhat elated. He was carrying a tablet in his free hand. Glyn Davies suspected he'd been up at his computer not only for the morning but most of the previous night.

"So you've got something already?" he said.

"Yes, sir. I think so. It wasn't too difficult, given I had the passwords. I dare say you and Sir Bernard could have done it yourselves without me."

Glyn Davies smiled, struck not for the first time by how often skilful people assume that what's obvious and easy for them must be so for every one else too. But all he said was, "I doubt it, Joseph. Anyway, let's look at what have you've got. Do you want to sit down? Or are you all right to walk with me for a bit?"

"Yes, sir, I can walk. It's a good day."

As a result of the car crash that killed his parents when he was thirteen, Joseph had spent many of his early years in a wheelchair. Then when he was in his twenties surgery and extensive physio-therapy had got him to a point where he was now able to walk about quite well with a stick. But still he had good days and bad days. Strikingly, the Chief Superintendent was one of the few people other than Verity who was allowed to refer to the matter without his being offended—a privilege that Glyn Davies valued very much.

So, with Joseph limping only slightly, they walked slowly by the white wooden posts along the edge of the car park. From their left came the constant buzz of late afternoon traffic from the Heavitree Road.

"Well sir," Joseph said, "first the bad news. I'm sorry to have to say it, but so far I've come across absolutely nothing that appears to relate to William Craig or to either of our murders."

Glyn Davies nodded. This was disappointing, but of course Sir Bernard had warned them.

"Have you told Detective Superintendent Cavaliere?"

"Not yet, sir. But I will."

"Right."

"The thing is, though, there's other material here that I think you and Sir Bernard ought to see immediately."

"Go on, Joseph."

"This section of MI5 that Sir Bernard is interested in—they've somehow got hold of a report that's dynamite. It's by the US GAO and—"

"The US GAO?"

"The United States' Government Accountability Office. That's the US government agency that audits the federal government."

"Okay."

"To cut a long story short, the sum of this report is that the most cutting-edge weapons in the US's military arsenal can be hacked quite easily using basic tools. In other words, even *I* could hack them, or someone like me. There are mission-critical cyber-vulnerabilities in virtually *every* US weapons systems tested between 2012 and 2017."

Glyn Davies whistled, but said nothing.

"The GAO's main finding is that there just isn't enough protection. On many of its systems the Pentagon hasn't even been bothering to change the passwords. And on one occasion—wait a minute, let me get this right—"

Joseph propped himself up on one of the posts, hooked his walking stick over his arm and with both hands now free scrolled down his tablet.

"—yes, here it is! On one occasion when it did change the password, a GAO operative guessed the new password *in nine seconds*. Another time, a team appointed by the GAO was able to gain actual control of a weapons system without any real difficulty, and then watch in real time as its operators realized something had happened and responded to the hackers."

He looked up at Glyn Davies.

"The copy of the report that I hacked has footnotes giving details of all these procedures, so anyone armed with this information could actually do it for themselves. Obviously I haven't tried them out, but I've looked at them carefully, and they appear to me to be authentic."

Davies nodded.

Joseph referred again to his tablet, scrolling down.

"Oh yes. According to the report it took a two-person GAO team only *one hour* to gain initial access to another weapons system, and then a mere day to gain full control. A number of other GAO appointed teams were able to copy, change or delete system data. One team downloaded *a hundred gigabytes* of information."

"That's a lot, I take it?"

Joseph looked up at him. "Oh yes, sir. That's a lot."

He went back to his tablet. "Again, details of the procedures involved are all fully footnoted. It appears to me that anyone who read and understood this report could do all this for themselves."

Glyn Davies shook his head.

"All this seems hardly credible," he said. "We're talking about the world's major military superpower."

"I think it's understandable. It takes a huge amount of time and energy to develop weapons systems like those we're talking about, and a lot of that time and energy are spent going over and over the same ground again and again, repeating or updating parts of earlier systems. And when you do that, it's easy to forget that your components and software are still based on original codes—which now are old and vulnerable—because of course as a developer you aren't thinking about codes. You're thinking about the system you're designing! And once you've actually got something working, even if someone does point out that the protection is old, it's got to be a big temptation to say, 'It isn't broken, so it doesn't need fixing!'"

"That's hardly an excuse."

"No, sir, it's not. And I admit the report says there are some very basic security flaws that could easily have been addressed by changing passwords and keeping software up-to-date. But it's all very human, I think."

Glyn nodded.

"So," he said, "Do we have any idea what the section in MI5 are proposing to do with all this information? Which I take it the Americans are not aware we have?"

"Apparently not. It appears to have been leaked to us from the US Senate's Armed Services Committee. Clearly the Senate committee's got a mole in its midst. But so far as I can see, the way *our* people are dealing with this material is where it all becomes especially weird. I think the section of MI5 that has this material isn't telling anyone about it. And I mean not *anyone*, not even anyone in MI5."

"And why, Joseph, do you think that?"

"Because of this second document which I also found among the section's papers," Joseph said, and as he did so offered his tablet to the Chief Superintendent, who looked a little surprised, but took it. "Both documents were securely emailed as attached documents to members of this section from the section head—whose name is Charles Saunders—and to no one else. They were accompanied, as you'll see, by instructions not to show them to or discuss them even with colleagues in the section.

"I think, sir," he added, "that it's best if you read Saunders' email and then the second document for yourself."

THIRTY-SEVEN

Near Exeter: the Winterbourne Memorial. About the same time.

"Here ma'am! We've found something!"

It was toward the end of the afternoon. It had been desperately hot work, but the searchers had more or less completed their twenty-metre circuit from the memorial, and Cecilia was beginning to think it was about time to call it a day, when the shout came.

By the time she arrived at the spot where the two young officers were waving, Bob Coulter was already there. There had been, to be sure, a couple of false alarms earlier on, but this time—

"I really think they've got something, ma'am," he said.

She peered down and nodded. A square of what looked like the rusty corner of a large box was sticking up from the newly disturbed earth.

"Let's have it out," she said.

It was actually an old-fashioned metal trunk, huge, battered, and rusting. It took them about twenty minutes to clear the ground round it of growth and roots, dig it up, and get it onto clear ground where they could deal with it. Ten to twelve minutes more were involved in working on the resistant locks and lid, gummed shut by years of dissolution. Finally it yielded and was forced open with a resounding crack.

Her stomach suddenly lurched.

"Sweet Jesus!" said someone standing beside her.

Someone else was sick.

One look told them all that they needed to know. Twisted and cramped into the dank, filthy space was the decaying carcase of what had once been a human being.

She gave a deep sigh.

"Set this up as a crime scene," she said. "And send for an MIT."

THIRTY-EIGHT

Exeter: the car park at Heavitree Police Station, a few minutes later.

The chief superintendent read carefully the email to which Joseph had directed him from the MI5 section head. It did indeed lay the restrictions on discussing the attachments exactly as Joseph had described.

Glyn Davies then turned to the second of the attached documents, which was headed: "Vulnerabilities of the U.K Election System" and subtitled, "Ways in which we may be assisted by the Main Directorate of the General Staff of the Armed Forces of the Russian Federation." His eyebrows shot up. The "Main Directorate", often known for short as GRU, was Russia's chief intelligence agency. People in the west had become generally aware of it in December 2016 when the White House put sanctions in place against it, accusing it of activities designed to disrupt and spread disinformation during the 2016 US presidential election.

He looked up for a moment at Joseph, who met his gaze and simply said, "You need to read it, sir."

Davies nodded, and went back to the document, which after further brief preamble went to what was clearly the point.

While it is true that the British voting system, depending as it does on paper ballots, is not so easily vulnerable to the skills of our Russian colleagues and their contacts as those of countries relying on electronic systems for the recording of votes, that does not mean that it is without vulnerabilities, or that elements of it cannot be hacked.

Such hacking in a British General Election or Referendum would, however, primarily involve targeting (1) external factors that affect people's choices, (2) their confidence in the system itself, lack of which might lead them not to bother to vote, and (3) finally, on the day itself, their actual physical ability to go out and vote.

The forms in which we may usefully undertake this targeting can therefore conveniently be divided into these three categories.

(1) Social engineering during the weeks immediately prior to an election or referendum. During this period, the important task would be to push news stories that support the views we wish to encourage via phishing campaigns or on social media. If this can be achieved on a large enough scale, there is plenty of evidence to suggest that it can have a significant impact on the outcome. It does not really matter whether the news stories are true or false, or even that they are particularly credible or convincing. A great many people do believe what they read, however absurd and far from the facts it may be — and this is especially the case when (for whatever reasons) they wish to believe it.*

(2) Disruption of national infrastructure systems in the period leading up to the election or referendum. The results of the recent Wannacry outbreak (12-15 May 2017) provide us with ample evidence of the chaos that this can cause. As a part of this, we would note various factors already present in the system. Recent polls indicate a general lack of trust in the government with regard to cyber security. Although some may have been influenced in coming to this view by general public awareness of the hacking that has dogged recent US and French elections, it is worth noting that polls suggest many people do not trust the UK government to protect the democratic process. This general lack of trust is certainly something that we can exploit.

(3) Disruption on the day of the election. At this point hacking

should focus on targeting and undermining external platforms that aid voting, including carpooling apps and websites that help voters identify their nearest polling stations. If we can stop enough people from voting, our work is done!

We need to concede that the dependence of so many British people for their knowledge of current affairs on the BBC and the Independent Television News, with their common general tradition (often to the point of absurdity) of ensuring that all points of view have a hearing, is a serious impediment to the spreading of the divisive artificial news that we wish to encourage. There is a much better chance of doing this in situations where a great many people take all their knowledge of public affairs from a single source that is heavily biased in a particular direction. Ideal, from this point of view, is the situation in the United States, where substantial portions of the population take all their information either from the Fox News Channel (right wing, conservative, inclined to be careless about facts), or else from MSNBC (left wing, progressive, usually careful about facts). Hence, in their view of public affairs, these two groups of the population are in effect living in different universes. It would be good if we could create such a situation in Britain, but unfortunately that does not at present seem likely. Let us not overlook, however, the increasing importance of social media: increasing numbers of people gather virtually all their news from Facebook (notoriously insecure) and Youtube (where blatantly false information frequently masquerades as news.) One sign that this has been having some useful effects is in the Brexit debate, where it becomes increasingly common for one side to refer to the side with which they disagree not as "wrong" or "mistaken" but as "traitors" if they are in favour of remaining in the European Union, or "racists" and "bigots" if they are in favour of leaving. This is, of course, exactly the kind of "debate" that we want to encourage.

The Chief Superintendent read this through a couple of times. Finally he looked up from the tablet and met Joseph's eye.

"What do *you* think is going on here?"

Joseph frowned.

"Pretty obviously, someone in our security services is planning to trade information about the American weapons systems with Russian security services in exchange for the Russians helping them get whomever they want elected at our next election."

Glyn Davies gave a faint smile.

"I agree with you," he said. "And so?"

"They're conspiring with a foreign power to undermine their own country, aren't they? Isn't that pretty well how the dictionary defines 'treason'?"

Glyn Davies and Joseph spoke with Cecilia later that afternoon. She was freshly returned to Heavitree from the excavations near the Winterbourne Memorial and naturally rather full of the discoveries they had made there.

It was surely strange to think that finding a murder victim should have anything about it that was good, but as it was, the simple fact that there had been a result—however gruesome—from one of their enquiries made it easier to communicate that there had not so far been a result from the other, at least not as far as their investigations into the death of Jack Hooper were concerned.

"But Joseph *has* been able to unearth some other materials that may be very useful to the security services," the chief superintendent said, "so we're still grateful to your informant for setting us off on that track, even though it hasn't led exactly where we hoped."

Cecilia responded with a stoic "Well that's good, isn't it, sir!" although he sensed—and suspected that Joseph did too—her frustration.

Thirty-Nine

An apartment in Westminster overlooking the River Thames.
Late afternoon of the same day.

The man in charge had arrived home from his office earlier than usual today, and now sat comfortably at the Chippendale desk in a big bay window looking out over what had once, in England's glory days, been the heart of an Empire, seething with energy and imagination.

He was here because there was work to be done—work that could not safely be done in Thames House. There were simply too many eyes to see and ears to hear. And he needed to write.

Writing was, indeed, a poor substitute for the reality of words uttered upon the breath with fire and passion. No one knew that better than he. There were moments when, for all the real progress they had made over recent months, he still longed for the cut and thrust of earlier days and the thrill of living rhetoric. Nothing could ever match the sensation of having men's eyes (and a few women's) fixed upon him, their bodies swaying with his every gesture, their souls pliable in his hands, ready to be moved as he chose, now to laughter, now to tears and finally, when it seemed right, to violent action.

He shook his head. He must face facts. What was needed now was the written word, not spoken. The movement as it grew would need texts, texts it could quote, texts it could rely on. And after all, had not his own first learning been through a text?

And such a text!

On impulse he reached across his desk for the first of a row of five immaculate, red leather-bound volumes that faced him: Theodor Mommsen's *History of Rome*, rendered into English in the vivid Victorian prose of William Purdie Dickson. Handling the volume with extreme care, he turned the pages until he came to the paragraph that had changed his life. He had first read it in a rather tired copy in the college library when he was sixteen. He read it again now as one who recites a creed, his lips silently forming the words before him:

> *By virtue of the law, that a people which has grown into a state absorbs its neighbours who are in political infancy, and a civilized people absorbs its neighbours who are in intellectual infancy--by virtue of this law, which is as universally valid and as much a law of nature as the law of gravity—*

He stopped reading for a moment. Why could so many not see this? By virtue of this law, then, ancient Rome had been

> *entitled to reduce to subjection the Greek states of the east which were ripe for destruction, and to dispossess the peoples of lower grades of culture in the west...*

Then came the essential claim, the assertion that even now was his cause and raison d'être:

> *England with equal right has in Asia reduced to subjection a civilization of rival standing but politically impotent, and in America*

and Australia has marked and ennobled, and still continues to mark and ennoble, extensive barbarian countries with the impress of its nationality.

Exactly.

He replaced the book in its stand, took up the enamelled silver Johnson and Boswell fountain pen that lay beside his blotter, and unscrewed the cap. It always pleased him when working at home to use the older technologies. He enjoyed the scent of real ink and the feel of paper, rich and creamy.

For a brief moment he gazed motionless at the blank sheet in front of him. Then he began to write.

Once he had started, the words came flowing and fast: lines of royal blue that streamed in swirls and loops across the cream surface before him. He drew initially on Mommsen—but what of that? If one is going to plagiarize, then plagiarize the best! But he surely had something to say on his own account.

Can our politicians and leaders not see that there are natural distinctions in the world—differences of function, divisions of labour, degrees of power and ability? These distinctions are laws of life—as inexorable as the laws of physics. One such distinction—and however much liberal theoreticians may try to evade it, all history on every continent points to it—is that it is the natural function of white races to rule, conquer others and be obeyed. This is not a matter of racism, but of simple observation.

Let us consider certain unarguable facts. Estimates vary according to various ways of gathering data and assessing it, but it may be stated with confidence that the white races account at most for one sixth, and very possibly for as little as one tenth, of the world's population. Yet it is members of this tiny minority who have been first to circumnavigate the globe, to orbit the world by spacecraft and to reach the moon, probing beyond it into the solar system. It is members of this minority who first have reached the North and South poles and plumbed the extreme depths of the oceans. It is members of this minority who have broken the sound barrier, unlocked the secrets of DNA and relativity, launched satellites, created automation and discovered electricity and nuclear energy. It is members of this minority who have invented railways, aircraft, submarines, photography, radio, telephones, television, computers and the microchip. In the face of all this achievement, how then can it reasonably be doubted that it is members of this minority, the white races, who are the most diligent and creative people on the planet, forever setting new goals of achievement and possibility that others merely follow?

For so long as we understood this self-evident truth, for so long as we accepted the need, indeed the duty and even (as the great Rudyard Kipling saw) the burden of white hegemony and leadership, there was some degree of order on the planet. And now that we deny it, what do we have? The Bard of Avon said it well:

Take but degree away, untune that string,

And, hark, what discord follows!

What we have is chaos. Western civilization, Christian civilization, has abandoned its calling. Islamists, Jews and Africans rear their heads where they ought not to be! These incomers breed with each other and, what is worse, with us! Where are our righteous Nehemiahs and Phineases, those among us who shall as of old strike down this lust and cast out its fruit?

He sat back, read through what he had written, and nodded.

It was a good beginning.

He was particularly pleased with rhetorical reference to Phineas and Nehemiah. It was always good to work in a reference to the Bible.

He licked his lips, and bent again to his task.

FORTY

Exeter: St Mary's Rectory, the same evening.

"I've good news," Cecilia said to Michael when they were settled for the evening on the sofa.

He was surprised. She'd not seemed full of good news earlier, when they were tending to the needs of the children and various other creatures.

But then at once she qualified it.

"Well," she said, "*sort of* good news. First of all, no luck so far with tracing a connection between our missing William Craig and the security services." She hesitated. "That's not good news, is it?"

"I don't think so."

She grimaced.

"I'm not being very clear, am I?"

"You've been clearer."

"Anyway, the sort-of-good news is this. Your mysterious informant was bang on target about the Winterbourne Memorial. We had a search party out this afternoon. They found something."

It's always comforting to know you haven't been wasting your wife's time, especially when your wife is a police officer on a murder enquiry.

But then—there was still that qualifying "sort of".

"I hope it was something helpful," he said cautiously.

Again Cecilia grimaced.

"It was rather horrible, actually. But in any case,"— she gave a little sigh—"it needed to be discovered."

"And?"

"And it was a body, rammed into a trunk."

"Oh, dear Lord."

"When we forced the trunk open one of the young PCs—Bob Carnell, I don't think you've met him yet, he's a nice lad—anyway, he was sick, and I can't say I blame him. I felt more or less the same. Maybe we all did. It had obviously been there for years and it was ghastly. Anyway, I'm quite sure what we've uncovered is a murder. So your information was important. Thank you."

Michael nodded. "So I suppose now Tom Foss and company get on with it?"

"That's right. They've already done all the photographing and videoing in situ, and taken the remains back to the mortuary. We'll know more tomorrow."

All of which now meant that Cecilia and company had *three* murders on their hands.

Exeter was starting to sound like Los Angeles.

FORTY-ONE

London: Thames House, Millbank. Friday, 14ᵗʰ September.

G lyn Davies wasted no time. He at once passed the documents and email that Joseph had discovered to Sir Bernard, who after examining them entirely agreed with him and Joseph about their significance.

Sir Bernard passed them to Ashley-Cooper the Acting Director.

And Ashley-Cooper without delay called in what was once known as Special Branch, but since 2006 had been referred to as Counter Terrorism Command or SO15. Their brief: to investigate the section of MI5 that was causing concern, and in particular, its chief, Charles Saunders.

The Counter Terrorism officers arrived at Thames House within hours of being alerted. They arrived without warning and insisted on speaking immediately with Saunders in his office. They did not beat about the bush.

"Mr Saunders," said the senior of the two, "concerns have been raised about a memorandum sent by you on the tenth of August of this year to members of the section you're in charge of. We need you to explain it to us."

Saunders glared at them.

"This is ridiculous," he said. "I am engaged with matters at the highest level of security directly affecting the safety and well-being of the United Kingdom. I can hardly believe I'm expected to interrupt that engagement in order to discuss with you *any* memorandum that may or may not have been sent internally in this building. And if you are really in possession of such a memorandum I would also demand to know how and by what right you came across it?"

But the officers were not to be deflected.

"Mr Saunders, whether you find it hard to believe or not, you *are* required to discuss this memo with us and you need to satisfy us that you sent it while acting within the terms of your responsibility to MI5."

"Very well. I take it you don't expect me to remember details of every memorandum I sent on a particular day several weeks ago. If you insist on acting out this farce you'll have to tell me what memorandum it was. Or at least—what was it about?"

"We need you to explain the contents of a secure email headed 'New Developments in Security' and two attached documents that went with it, headed respectively 'G.A.O. Report on U.S. Weapons Systems: Vulnerabilities' and 'Vulnerabilities of the U.K. Election System.'"

There was a pause.

"And is that it? That's why you have interrupted my morning? To talk about that?"

"Yes."

Saunders gazed at them for a few seconds. Then, muttering irritably, "This beggars belief," he bent forward and pressed a button.

"Sir?"

"Barnes, bring me hard copy of documents five and six in the Elections File."

"Yes sir. It will take me a couple of minutes."

"I will wait."

The three sat in silence.

Saunders opened up a black leather document case that lay in front of him, removed from it an official looking document with what appeared to be a coat of arms at its head, and proceeded to read it.

After a few minutes a secretary came in, placed a folder on the desk and withdrew silently.

Saunders looked up from his document and with one hand pushed the folder toward the two Counter Terrorism officers.

"I suggest you look at those," he said, and returned to his reading.

They opened the folder and found themselves faced with a series of forms for assessment and evaluation based on "recent trial and test documents" that had been sent to various members of the section that Saunders headed—documents referred to by title—"GAO Report on US Weapons Systems: Vulnerabilities" and "Vulnerabilities of UK Election System".

There were a series of questions. How had members of the section reacted to these documents? Had they objected to or been concerned about proposals in them? If so, which proposals had caused them to object or feel concern? And why? And how had they handled those objections or concerns? Had they breached the instruction not to discuss the proposals with anyone, even their colleagues? Had they taken their objections or concerns to a senior officer? Had they breached confidentiality even further and gone outside the system? Alternatively, had they *not* objected to the proposals or expressed any concerns? And if so, why not? Had they appeared willing to go along with the actions proposed in the documents?

The two interviewers read through this material with increasing uncertainty and confusion—uncertainty and confusion that were not eased when Saunders finally looked up from his reading and said, "As you see, when completed by individual members of section, based on their reactions to the materials you have seen, these forms are—or at least, were—scheduled to be sent to our personnel department for evaluation and assessment."

"That certainly appears to be the case," said one of the interviewers hesitantly, looking again at the top of the first sheet.

"It *is* the case," Saunders said.

"I have," he continued, "for some time been personally concerned about the priorities and objectives of some of the members of this section. I am sure that all regard themselves as patriots, but this assessment seemed to me to be a way of winkling out those whose understanding of patriotism might not concur with the views of the government. I believe it would have succeeded."

"Did anyone else know of this planned assessment, sir?"

"Of course someone else knew. I informed the acting Director General that I was planning it, and why, and he concurred. I am sure he has copies of the memoranda that we exchanged, as do I."

"Did you send him copies of *all* the documents you used in the assessments, and the questions to go with them?"

Saunders sighed, as a teacher trying to be patient with a particularly dull student.

"I kept him informed of my *strategy* and of its *goal*, officer. Certainly I could and would have provided details of my procedures if asked, but I was not asked. Nor did I expect to be. In case you had not noticed, let me point out that there are more than four thousand people working for MI5. One can hardly expect the Director General to have time to take detailed note of every procedure in every section."

He gazed at them for a moment, then shook his head slowly, replaced the document he had been reading in its case, and closed the case.

He sat back in his large desk chair.

"If," he said, "whoever sent you had had the good sense or

even the common courtesy to come and ask me about this matter personally and at once, I could have furnished all this information to you immediately and set your minds at rest. As it is, your blundering presence now, surely known to everyone in the section if not in the building, has not only wasted my time and yours, but also quite possibly corrupted any results we might have looked for from these surveys."

He paused a moment, then continued quietly but firmly, "The irony is, we are all well aware that Counter Terrorism is not being effective. The Westminster Bridge attack in March last year, the Manchester Arena bombing in May, the London Bridge attack in June, the Finsbury Park Mosque attack, the recent attacks in Salisbury on Sergei Skripal and his daughter Yulia—I mention only events that must obviously come to the mind of any member of the public who follows the news at all—all represent failure to fulfil or even come close to your brief. And yet you have the gall to throw away taxpayers' money by launching investigations into people like me!"

Again there was a pause.

"So," one of the Counter Terrorism officers said, "this was all just a way to test your own department's loyalty?"

"Exactly. You seem to have got it at last. Now, do you have something else that you wish to show me? Do you have other questions to ask? Do you intend to charge me with anything?"

The two Counter Terrorism men looked blankly at each other.

After a moment Saunders said, "Evidently not!"

He lent forward and again touched the buzzer on his intercom. "Sir?"

"Barnes, come in here, will you."

He turned back to the men from Counter Terrorism.

"This enquiry is a disgrace. Since you clearly have nothing further to present and no charges to bring, I suggest the pair of you end this charade and find some other way to amuse yourselves."

His secretary had entered while he was speaking, and now stood quietly by. Saunders turned to her.

"Barnes, these men are leaving. Show them out. I have work to do, even if they haven't."

FORTY-TWO

Exeter: Heavitree Police Station. Saturday, 15ᵗʰ September.

Sir Bernard, in passing the documents discovered by Joseph to Ashley-Cooper, had explicitly advised him *not* to act hastily, but rather to watch and wait. Needless to say, he was furious that his replacement's precipitous action would undoubtedly have achieved exactly the result he had been trying to avoid—if there were seditious elements at work within MI5, it would have alerted them to the fact that someone was on to them.

Sir Bernard's own embarrassment when he was obliged to pass all this on to Glyn Davies was evident.

"I fear that not only have I been of no assistance at all to you in the murder investigations that your team are working on, I have also created a shambles of the investigation that we were supposed to be having here into rogue elements."

The chief superintendent could hardly disagree. The thing had been a comprehensive disaster.

"I suppose," he said, "that this fellow Saunders *had* communicated his intentions to Ashley-Cooper, as he said he had?"

"He had, at least formally. I asked to see the memos myself. Saunders' memo is *very* cleverly written in terms that certainly now cover his arse but are bland enough not to have raised red flags when they were sent. And the response from Ashley-Cooper's office giving the go-ahead is simply routine. If you ask me, I doubt Ashley-Cooper had even read it. In any case it was clear to me that he didn't really remember it. If he had, he'd surely have linked it to the documents that our friend Joseph had discovered and that we passed to him. I think I can just about forgive that. There *are* literally hundreds of memos circulating every day."

Glyn Davies frowned. What Sir Bernard's loyalty to his deputy forbade him to say was obvious: he could *not* forgive the over-hasty action that had for the moment ruined their chances of actually catching Saunders out. Glyn Davies, however, was bound by no such loyalty. Rather, he felt bound to face a darker possibility.

"Sir, I suppose we can trust Ashley-Cooper himself, can we? You're sure there's no chance his mishandling of this was deliberate?"

There was a long pause.

Finally Sir Bernard said, "That possibility has occurred to me. I don't *think* it's the case, but I grant it might be. I've tipped off a couple of people in Counter Terrorism whom I trust. They'll be watching him. For what it's worth they have authority to tap his communications and that's being done—though of course anyone who's up to no good these days knows to communicate through a throwaway mobile. But without any substantial evidence, or at least until we have some, I'm not sure what else we can do."

"Thank you, sir." Again Glyn Davies nodded, relieved to learn that the eye of suspicion was not simply ignoring the person who appeared to him to be an obvious suspect.

In the meantime, he had his own problems. There now fell to him the embarrassing task of passing on to Joseph the news of what had happened—with its evident corollary that Joseph's own hours of skilful and painstaking work had, in effect, been wasted.

FORTY-THREE

Exeter: the Police Mortuary. The same morning.

Three of the tiled walls and the tiled floor that slanted toward the centre were white. The figures moving quietly about the long room wore white coats and the lights above them shone white and cold, gleaming on stainless steel operating tables down the centre and white refrigeration units that lined the fourth wall. As always when she visited the mortuary, Cecilia had the bizarre feeling that somehow she had become part of an old black and white movie.

The body they had found at the Winterbourne Cross was now laid out on one of the tables, what was left of its face set in a ghastly smile. This would definitely be a horror movie.

"Our estimate," Tom Foss said, "is that he was a young man, not more than twenty, and that he was killed about twenty years ago. Maybe a little more."

"Is there any chance of an ID?" she asked.

"Actually," he said, "there is, and without too much trouble. There's a wallet. It's disintegrating, of course, but the credit cards and library card in it are all perfectly readable. According to them his name was Gladstone S. Walker. There's also a mobile phone.

We might be able to get more info off that. For confirmation if we need it there's also dentistry."

"And the manner of death?"

"Well, the body has multiple fractures to multiple bones and his skull is fractured. I'd say the fellow was certainly savagely beaten—probably kicked around viciously by a number of people—before he died."

Cecilia nodded, flinching mentally at the sudden picture of what the young man's last moments must have been like. How could people do this kind of thing to each other?

"But," Tom Foss continued, "the beating isn't what killed him. His injuries were serious, and they might have proved fatal in the long run. But there was no long run."

"So what did he die from?"

"A bullet to the head: virtually an execution. I suppose for some reason whoever it was stopped beating him up and just did it: shot him." He paused. "The thing is—the bullet."

"Yes?"

"It's a 2.7 mm Kolibri. The same kind of bullet as killed your young fellow on the beach."

"The same gun? For two murders twenty years apart?"

"We haven't sent it to ballistics yet, so we don't know it's the same gun. But it might be. After all, it's not as if there are a great many guns about that fire that kind of ammunition. Or ever were, come to that."

Cecilia nodded. If it was just a coincidence, it was one hell of a coincidence.

But still, what we can't show, we don't know.

"All right then, Tom. Let's get it to ballistics."

FORTY-FOUR

Heavitree Police Station. Early afternoon.

Joseph was already having a bad day. This was the second week-end in a row when he'd felt obliged to work, and overlong hours, it seemed, were finally taking their toll. He had a headache, his back was hurting and streaks of pain went up his left leg every few minutes. Nothing seemed to be helping—neither his painkillers nor his special chair. He had changed his adjustable workstation to every position he could think of, but it did not seem to make any difference whether he sat or stood.

It was in the midst of this that he had been obliged to hear the latest bad news from the Chief Superintendent.

It hardly improved his mood.

"The documents I found are real," he said to Verity some time later. "And that fellow Saunders is guilty as hell. I'm sure of it. But they're dealing with a clever man. He had his backup story all prepared in case somebody rumbled him. And now he's been forewarned they're onto him, and they can watch him all they like. It won't do any good. For the time being he'll keep himself squeaky clean. We can be sure of that!"

Verity nodded.

"And *that*," he added, "is assuming he stays around at all. Now he knows we're onto him I can see him simply disappearing altogether."

Nursing her big blue and yellow mug full of tea, Verity perched herself where she used to perch in the days when they were first spending time together—where he still liked her to perch, on his desk beside his workstation and the computer.

"So what else do we know about him?" she asked.

"Who? Saunders?"

"Yes. For instance, what's his other name? I assume he's got one."

"It's Charles. Charles Edward Saunders."

"And?"

"He's very top drawer: old Sussex family with pots of money. King's Scholar at Eton, open—"

"That's interesting."

He stared at her. "What?"

"*Another* Eton King's Scholar!" she said. "William Craig was one too. Remember? But go on about Saunders."

"All right—well, open scholarship to Balliol, read English, got a first, joined the civil service, heading for the top. But then there was a family tragedy. His parents and sister died in a hotel fire in Switzerland in 2001. According to all accounts he was lucky to escape with his life. Following that he seems to have decided to change everything. He abruptly left the Civil Service, and joined MI5 in 2002."

"No other relatives?"

"There's a surviving grandmother who's very frail. Apparently she suffers from senile dementia. She's in a residential care home in Yorkshire."

"And that's it?"

"The other grandparents on both sides died some years ago."

She nodded. "That *is* a sad story." She paused. "So when was Saunders at Eton?"

Joseph checked his computer. "1985 to 1990."

"And when was our other King's Scholar there? William Craig?"

Joseph stared at her for a moment. It suddenly dawned on him where she might be going with this.

But that, surely, would be too much to hope?

He peered again at his computer.

He typed something in.

A slow smile spread across his face.

"Verity Jones, you are not only gorgeous, you are a genius. *William Craig and Charles Saunders were in the same class.*"

Which meant that without resort to ingenious hacking into secret data or the use of any other strange and unusual methods of enquiry, but simply by exploring information that was a matter of public record, they had found a connection between the elusive William Craig and Charles Saunders of MI5—which was as good as to say, they had found a connection between their own case and the security services.

Joseph had no difficulty at all in forgiving Verity when she smirked.

FORTY-FIVE

Joseph and Verity had phoned Cecilia on Saturday evening to tell her about the possible link between William Craig and Charles Saunders—news which had cheered her considerably. What was more, its timing meant that she had the rest of the weekend to think about it.

Still elated and with a couple of half-formed new ideas in her head, she began her day on Monday by seeing whether she might talk by phone with either of the two officers from Counter Terrorism who'd been sent to interview Saunders at Thames House. Somewhat to her surprise one of them was available.

"What was your general impression of him?" she said.

"Prissy, pompous little bugger," was the response. "His office was huge and classy, and so dam' tidy you felt you ought to eat your own fingerprints. He had this huge, polished desk with *one* document on it, right in the middle, absolutely square on. And after he'd finished looking at it, he carefully put it back in *exactly* the same position he'd picked it up from. I tell you, I think I'd go mad if I had to work with a bloke like that.

"Mind you," he added after a pause, "he's clever. There's no denying that." He chuckled ruefully. "He had us dead to rights. Made mincemeat of us. So my advice is, anyone who wants to catch out Mr Charlie Saunders had better get up *very* early in the morning! I mean to say—with what we had I thought we had *him* dead to rights. But he had an answer for everything."

After this conversation, which she actually found rather illuminating, Cecilia spent the next part of her morning dealing with administration. She was of course delighted when the intercom on her desk buzzed and interrupted her.

"It's Dr Foss, ma'am," said the operator. "Are you free to talk to him?"

"Certainly I'm free to talk to Dr Foss!" she said, dismissing administration with an airy mental wave.

For once Tom Foss sounded excited, and did not waste time on any dramatic pauses.

"Cecilia," he said, "I've got the ballistics report. Our murder on the beach and our murder in 1994—the bullets on both occasions were fired from the same gun."

"*Really?*"

"Yes, really."

"Tom that's brilliant. Thank you."

"And there's another thing," he said.

"Yes, Tom?"

"There are some new techniques for getting DNA evidence that are very effective, and using them we've managed to obtain traces of another DNA from the back of the collar of the deceased's shirt—DNA that isn't the deceased's, I mean."

"That's interesting. No matches to anything, I suppose? You've run it though all the databases?"

"First thing we did. No such luck. But I dare say the way it's placed tells us a bit more about how the fellow died."

He stopped. She waited.

"It looks to me," he said quietly, "as though at some point

he was gripped from behind by his shirt collar. I'd guess it was to keep him from moving while he was shot in the back of the head."

Cecilia felt physically sick.

FORTY-SIX

Exeter: Heavitree Police Station, that afternoon.

The team met in Cecilia's office that afternoon at two.
There was plenty of new information for them to share,
including three more pieces that came to her minutes before the
meeting.

First, that a young man called Gladstone Stewart Walker had
been reported missing in Exeter on the fifth of June, 1994, having
last been seen on the second, and that his mother Mrs Leoma
Walker was still living in Exeter.

Second, that a certain Francis Hawke-Genn, who had taught
classics to William Craig and Charles Saunders while they were at
Eton, and for one year had been their form master, was now living
in retirement in a cottage at Ashbourne in the Dales.

Third, that the Met had so far drawn a blank in their efforts to
find out what had happened to Robert Cornellisen.

"So," Cecilia said, standing by the crowded whiteboard and
summing up at the end of a long session, "where are we? Our two
murders have now blossomed into three, and our missing person
is still missing."

"Pretty staggering that our decades old murder and our days

old murder were both with the same gun," Headley said. "That's surely a marker, if we can work out how to read it."

"Find the gun and we've found our killer," Tom said.

"But let's not forget Jack Hooper was bludgeoned to death, not shot," Verity said. "We've got *three* murders—somehow linked, I admit—but with *two* completely different MOs."

"That's true," Cecilia said, "but let's also not forget Jack Hooper was killed by a professional assassin whose identity we know. Maybe the shooter in the other two cases is the person that hired Marcel Gagnon in Jack Hooper's case."

"If so, then said shooter has now killed the professional assassin's brother," Verity said. "This gets weirder and weirder."

"But of course Tom's right," Headley said. "It would be good to find that gun. Has anyone talked to Bob Coulter about the possibilities of tracing it?"

"I have," Joseph said. "He points out that as a working pistol a Kolibri semi-automatic would be illegal in private ownership in the UK anyway. But it can probably get by if it's treated as an antique weapon. I've got a couple of my blokes looking over sales in Britain over the last couple of decades, but so far no luck. The thing is, it's *quite* rare, but it's not *so* rare that it's easy to find."

He paused.

"What I'm equally anxious to follow up on," he said, "is the new information we now have about William Craig and Charles Saunders. Maybe Saunders knows where Craig is now? Maybe he's even in touch with him? Wouldn't that be a turn up!"

"From what I've heard, I don't exactly see Saunders co-operating with another police interview to discuss that or anything else," Headley said. "Not if the tale I've heard of his interview with Anti-Terrorism is even half true!"

"Neither do I," Joseph said. "No more interviews with Saunders until we've actually got something on him! But could you interview this retired schoolmaster who knew them both at Eton?"

"I think we should," Cecilia said. "Tom, Headley, I'd like you to do that. A free all expenses paid trip to beautiful Ashbourne, jewel of the Dales!"

The two looked at each other and grinned.

"Does all expenses include beer?" Tom asked.

"And of course we'll need a good dinner in a top local restaurant the night before," Headley added, "just to create the right impression. We don't want the Devon and Cornwall constabulary to look cheapskate."

"Don't push your luck. If we're feeling generous we may cover you for a sardine sandwich and a cup of coffee in a lay-by. Now what else?"

"Gladstone Walker's mother," Verity said.

"Yes!" Cecilia said. "Absolutely! Mrs Leoma Walker. We have her address? And she's in Exeter?"

Verity nodded.

"So—let's you and me go see her," Cecilia said. "Will you fix an appointment for us?"

"On it, ma'am," Verity said, tactfully ignoring her superior officer's grammar.

FORTY-SEVEN

Exeter: a residential street. The following afternoon,
Tuesday, 18th September.

The Walkers' house was number thirty-six in a quiet residential street, tree-lined with neat gardens and modest but pleasant detached houses built, for the most part, in the sixties. Cecilia nodded with approval at a shiny and obviously much loved sky-blue Fiat Seicento parked in front of number thirty-six.

"Clearly they have impeccable taste in cars," she said.

"Yes, ma'am," Verity said philosophically.

Leoma Walker was a large, pleasant lady who had surely to be in her sixties but could have passed for forty-five. She truly was (as Jane Austen might have put it) "of substantial size", and Cecilia could not help wondering whether she drove the Seicento and if so how she fitted into it. When Cecilia and Verity announced themselves she at once invited them in, past a framed cross stitch in the hall which announced "Blessed are the pure in heart for they shall see God" and into a small sitting room with large, comfortable chairs, flat screen television and a lithograph over the mantelpiece of a bearded man in a long white robe who was standing up in a boat in the midst of heavy seas and pointing at the sky. Other men with beards and loincloths were lurching round him. It must be Jesus calming the storm, Cecilia decided.

"Would you like a cup of tea?" Leoma Walker said. "And a chocolate digestive biscuit?"

"Yes, please," Verity said promptly.

"Thank you," Cecilia said.

Leoma Walker looked at them for a moment and then said to Cecilia, "A little milk and no sugar for you," and to Verity, "Quite a lot of milk and two sugars for you! Is that right?"

They both laughed.

"That's brilliant!" Verity said. "How did you know?"

Their host chuckled. "I didn't. But I usually guess right!"

The tea arrived in royal family commemorative mugs. Cecilia had Kate and William's wedding, Verity had Meghan and Harry's and Mrs Walker had Princess Charlotte.

"The royals are always doing something new," she said, "so if a mug gets broken you can easy replace it. It's very convenient of them!"

The appearance of the chocolate biscuits was followed by the appearance of a medium-sized brown dog who came up to Cecilia and lent against her hopefully.

"This is Disraeli. He's not allowed chocolate though he thinks he should be. He's supposed to be here to guard us. But if anyone breaks in the chief danger will be that he may lick them to death."

Leoma Walker was entirely Caribbean in appearance, but in her speech pure Devon. "My mother came over in nineteen sixty as a young nurse to work in the health service, and I was born here. I followed in her footsteps and I've worked in hospitals in Exeter all my life. Now my daughter Aletheia is a doctor at the Royal Devon and Exeter. We've been to Jamaica for holidays and to see family, but we reckon we're Devonians now!"

The story that Cecilia and Verity had to tell her was evidently distressing, and Cecilia had been prepared for an outburst of grief when she heard of the discovery of her son's body. But Mrs Walker took the news with quiet dignity.

Of course Cecilia had read the decades old missing persons report. But still she was interested to hear about Gladstone Walker's disappearance from his mother's point of view.

"It was the day after his eighteenth birthday. Gladstone went out with friends. They told us he went to a fish and chip shop because he fancied some chips, but then he didn't meet up with them again afterwards. Unfortunately, though he was not a bad-hearted boy, he was always a bit of a wild one. He'd quite often stay out overnight or even two or three nights with his friends without telling us, and then turn up again afterwards full of cheerfulness and apologies for forgetting to call. So at first we weren't worried. But then after four days we got anxious and went to the police and reported him missing. I think they did their best, but, well, we never saw him again."

That's generous, Cecilia thought. The truth was, reading the police report, she'd been disturbed from the start when she saw that the man in charge had been Detective Superintendent Timothy Barnwell, an officer who'd later turned out to be corrupt. Aside from that, the report was not impressive as a record of police work. It was clear that once he'd learned the young man had a habit of going missing and had always turned up previously, Barnwell had been happy enough to conclude he would probably turn up now, and to leave it at that. The police had gone through the motions of a search, but nothing more.

She sighed.

"I'm very sorry, Mrs Walker," she said.

"That's all right, child. I did my grieving many years ago. But I would like to see Gladstone if that is possible."

Cecilia thought of the gruesome remains lying in the police morgue.

"Of course you may see him, Mrs Walker. Though I feel I ought to say... it's just that... it will be very hard. You won't recognize him. And you may not want to remember him as he is now."

"He is my son. I know the body is only a shell, but this body once held Gladstone's soul and I once held it. However it is now, I need to say goodbye. I think my daughter and our pastor will come with me to see him if that is allowed."

"Certainly it's allowed Mrs Walker," Cecilia said. "Please, let's try to arrange this in any way that would be best for you."

When they got back to Heavitree, Joseph was waiting for them.

"I've just found something rather remarkable," he said, "and frankly I can't imagine why the police didn't take it into consideration when Gladstone Walker was originally reported missing."

"What's that?" Cecilia said.

"There was a rally of the extreme right in Winterbourne village on the second of June 1994—the last night the boy was seen alive. There was stuff about it—the rally, I mean—in all the papers. The *Express and Echo* had a lead on it and it even made the nationals. National Front, British Nationalists, British Union, the whole lot! Some idiot had let the Winterbourne parish hall to them without checking who they were. Of course there was an almighty row afterwards."

"And yet when a black boy suddenly disappeared on just the night these folk were in town, no one thought to ask whether they might have had anything to do with it?"

"Apparently not."

"Sheer incompetence," Verity said.

"Or worse," Cecilia muttered.

"Of course," said the ever-logical Verity, "we don't actually *know* that the right wing lot did it."

"No," Cecilia said, "we don't. But I can think of someone who might."

FORTY-EIGHT

Ashbourne, Derbyshire. The following morning:
Wednesday, 19ᵗʰ September.

It was not the best of days in the world's affairs. A typhoon was devastating southern China. The American president's nominee for Supreme Court judge was being accused of sexual assault. Strawberries containing hidden needles were being discovered in supermarkets in Australia. And here in the United Kingdom the government was of course in the midst of its by now customary chaos over Brexit, at a stage where with varying degrees of glee and detail pundits and gurus from every side were pointing to a mounting possibility that the United Kingdom might actually crash out of the European Union without any kind of agreement or arrangement at all—a scenario offering possibilities for economic and social disaster on which said pundits held forth at length.

Regardless of all this, Headley and Tom, inspired no doubt by the optimism and good spirits of youth, enjoyed an excellent breakfast at the George and Dragon in Ashbourne. In spite of Detective Superintendent Cavaliere's threats and caveats, the breakfast was on expenses, as were supper and their rooms at the inn the night before, although they had paid for their own beer.

All this now behind them, they set out to see Mr Francis Hawke-Genn, who when they contacted him earlier had graciously invited them to take coffee with him at ten o'clock.

They arrived on the dot and were greeted by Mr Hawke-Genn himself, a slender, slightly stooping, gently mannered man wearing pince-nez and a dark suit with waistcoat and bowtie. He glanced briefly at their identification, invited them in and presented them to his wife, a white haired lady as gentle in manner as he, who showed them to a tiny sitting room and served them coffee by way of an elegant Victorian coffee set.

When the two police officers were settled to the best of their hosts' ability, Mrs Hawke-Genn excused herself. After she had left the room her husband sat back in his chair.

"So how may I assist you gentlemen?" he said.

"We were wondering, sir," Headley said, "whether from your years of teaching you remember anything of two King's Scholar's who were at the college from 1985 to 1990, William Craig and Charles Saunders? It may be important in a case we are working on."

Hawke-Genn nodded and gave a rather sad little smile. "Indeed, I do. I remember them quite well."

"Could you tell us about them?"

"I can tell you what I recall."

"And would you mind, sir, if we recorded what you can tell us? Our superior officers will want to listen to it."

"I would not mind in the least." He paused, while they set their phones to record, and then continued. "We used to call Craig and Saunders 'the terrible twins' but that was a just a joke. In truth they weren't terrible at all. They *were* close friends, however. They sat together in class when they could, and were almost always together at other times. Both of them were, of course, rather brilliant, which meant, I suppose, that they gave to each other a certain intellectual stimulation that many of their fellows could not. And they actually looked rather alike. I dare say they could have been taken for real twins, not identical of course, just fraternal. But they had the same build—both of them quite small for their age—and the same fair hair."

He paused again. "Is this helpful? Is this the sort of thing you want to know? My wife will tell you that it is very dangerous to encourage me to start talking about the days of my youth. I may never stop!"

Headley and Tom nodded vigorously.

"Absolutely sir," Headley said, "this is exactly the sort of thing we'd like to know."

Francis Hawke-Genn smiled. "Well then, if you find it useful!" He paused, seeming to gather his thoughts. "In their personal circumstances," he continued at last, "the two boys were very different. Young Craig had no family—or at least, none that acknowledged him. His fees and all his expenses were always paid and everything he needed was always provided promptly, but the source of this bounty was never revealed. I suspected then, and I suspect now, that he was the offspring of some wealthy and theoretically respectable person who was decent enough to see that the child did not want for things material but for some reason chose not to acknowledge him. But of course that is just my speculation."

Headley and Tom both nodded.

"Young Saunders was in a very different position. He had a wonderful family—generous, warm, and outgoing—a beautiful elder sister—all the boys fell in love with her when she came to see him at half term—and two delightful parents. And I may say they were all extremely kind to Craig. After the first year as I recall he spent all his holidays with them, and was treated by them as virtually a part of their family."

He paused.

"I would not be misunderstood. The two boys were also in

some ways quite different from each other. Thus, Saunders was bouncy and noisy and enjoyed a joke, whereas Craig was clipped and precise and struggled, I think, to find a sense of humour. Saunders was, I believe, very good for him in that respect. Again, Saunders was utterly untidy: his desk, his books, everything always appeared to be in chaos. Whereas Craig was invariably meticulous: a place for everything and everything in its place. But still, they got on well. And both were excellent scholars, in their own way."

He sighed.

"It all ended sadly, of course."

The detectives looked at him encouragingly.

"After leaving here," he continued, "they followed very different paths. Saunders went up to Balliol, obtained a first in the Honours School of English Literature and joined the civil service, where he continued to do well. But then there was an awful family tragedy: a fire at the hotel where they were staying on holiday in Switzerland. His parents and his sister all died. Saunders was the only one of his family to survive."

He shook his head.

"I fear that terrible experience must have changed him completely, poor fellow. He had up until that time been quite prominent among the Old Etonians, always organizing things—charitable efforts, that sort of thing—and invariably coming back to the college for major events. But since the death of his family, not once! I haven't seen him since the tragedy and I don't know anyone else who has either. That must have been ten, fifteen, no, more than fifteen years ago. He even changed his job. I think he's still working for the government, but now in the security services. I dare say that may be better for someone who chooses to be a recluse. But it's sad for those of us who knew him, and it must be sad for him."

He fell silent.

"Do you know any more of William Craig, sir?" Headley asked.

"Ah, yes. A very different history from that of his friend, but also a sad history, and in the things that matter most, I would say, even sadder: Saunders lost his family, but Craig seems to have lost his soul." He sighed. "To cut a long story short, after leaving us the boy seems to have gone completely off his head. Instead of going up to Oxford as was expected—he had a place at the House and I dare say he might have got a scholarship if he'd tried: he was certainly bright enough—anyway, he abandoned all that and joined some awful fascist group, sort of Mosleyites I suppose, declaring white men to be the master race, rattling on about blood and soil, all that sort of nonsense. I can't imagine where he acquired such ideas. Certainly not from anyone here! Anyway, however he learnt it, he and his fascist friends were involved in some terrible violence against people they didn't like—wrong colour, wrong religion, whatever. Eventually they firebombed a house in London and killed an entire Jewish family. They were caught for that, thank God, and most of Craig's fellow criminals went to prison. But Craig himself disappeared. I don't believe anyone's heard from him since. Certainly I haven't. I believe the police are still looking for him, at least in theory?"

He looked at Headley and Tom, who both nodded.

"That's right, sir," said Tom. "It's still technically an open case."

"Well," said Hawke-Genn, "for what it's worth, it's my belief Craig suddenly realized the enormity of what he'd done and it was all too much for him. He couldn't face life in prison so he went off quietly somewhere by himself and did the only decent thing. But of course that's just my speculation."

FORTY-NINE

HM Prison Belmarsh. The same afternoon.

"You mean the West Country Rally for England," George Williams said, broadly echoing his brother. "That's what they called it."

"When they killed a black man?" Verity said.

"That's right. I wasn't there myself. It was in '94 and me and my brother, we didn't join 'til '96. But even a couple of years later they were all still talking about it."

"And what about the black man?"

"Oh yes, him, poor fucker. Well, as we heard it, it was like this. A load of our lot was walking through Exeter before the rally, when a couple of them saw the darkie buying chips in a chip shop. So they wait until he come out and then grab him and take him out to Winterbourne where they're having the main meeting. After the meeting they drag him out to some deserted spot near the woods and rough him up. And then Craig kills him."

There was brutal simplicity about this narrative, but so far as it went it covered the facts as they knew them—and then some.

"Do you know anyone we could talk to who was actually there? Someone who saw it?" Verity asked.

He paused, considering, and after a moment shook his head.

"Not that I know of. It was Sam Slater, who was British Union before us but got bird same time as we did, he was the bloke who was actually there. He used to talk about it a lot, 'specially when he was pissed. We all heard him. But he died last year so you can't talk to him."

Verity nodded.

"Can you remember if Sam Slater ever described what happened at the rally in a bit more detail? " Verity said. "I mean, about them killing the black man?"

George frowned.

"'Far as I can remember he said at first our lot just kept calling the lad 'dirty nigger' and such and generally roughing him up and banging him around. But then apparently the darkie suddenly got free and got in a couple of good punches of his own and knocked a couple of the fuckers down. So then the rest of them didn't like that so they all completely lost it and charged in on him all at once and beat him down and kicked him round. I guess he could fight two or three of them, but not ten or twenty."

"But you said it was Craig who actually killed him," Cecilia said. "How did that happen? Did he put in the final kick or something?"

Williams gave a sardonic chuckle.

"Oh no! William Craig would have been much too smooth to be doing anything like that, getting his hands dirty—or his feet! Sam said he just shouted something like, 'Hold the nigger still for me!' or something like that, and those fuckers had him kneeling on the ground with about four of them holding on to him and then Craig brings out a gun—and he steps up behind the darkie, grabs him by his collar, presses the gun against his woolly black head and shoots him dead, straight through the back of the head. So then they all give a great cheer. That's how Sam Slater told it, anyway."

"Did he ever mention what they did with the body?" Cecilia asked. "Maybe just left it there?"

Williams looked puzzled. "Not sure. I think maybe Slater said they buried it so the cops wouldn't find it. But I ain't sure."

Cecilia exchanged a look with Verity, who nodded. They'd started their interviews by asking the prisoners whether they knew anything of an extreme right-wing rally at the village of Winterbourne near Exeter in June 1994, in which a black man had been killed. They'd deliberately not said anything about their discovery of Gladstone Walker's body or about the state of it. Nor had they said anything about how he died.

The reassuring fact about what they'd just heard, even though it was not from an actual eyewitness, was that in all main points it agreed with what they'd already learned from forensics—even down to details of the victim having been shot in the back of the head. Perhaps then they might also believe what it told them that was new—namely, that it been the illusive William Craig who actually pulled the trigger?

"Tell me," Cecilia said, "if we ever managed to get William Craig into custody and charge him, would you be willing to tell a court all this? Would you be willing to identify him and to tell them what Sam Slater told you?"

"Would I grab a chance to screw that little fucker like we all got screwed? You bet your life I would. And so would my brother. And we'd tell them how Craig knew all about the Jews we firebombed that night, and was all for us doing it—as he was. That ain't nothin' but the truth."

Cecilia nodded. His brother had already said much the same.

"Why?" he said. "Do you think you can catch him? After all this time?"

She met his eye.

"I honestly don't know, Mr Williams," she said. "But I can tell you we're going to have a dam' good try."

"It'd be hearsay evidence," Verity said as they drove away from the prison.

"It would be first hand hearsay, and the original witness is dead, so it would be admissible," Cecilia said.

From time to time Michael would quote Elie Wiesel, who was one of his heroes—" When you listen to a witness, you become a witness."

But Verity was shaking her head.

"Let's say the story is true," she said, "and personally I believe it is. Even so, the court is going to hear it from a convicted criminal with an obvious and admitted grudge against the defendant. What do you think any half-decent defending counsel is going to do with that?"

Cecilia sighed.

Verity had a point.

They would need more.

A lot more.

FIFTY

The team met, and once more pooled its information. Cecilia listened fascinated to the account of William Craig and Charles Saunders given by their old form master. She and Verity shared the new revelations about Gladstone Walker's death stemming from their visit to Belmarsh Prison.

But life was going on.

A recurring fact of life for everyone involved in policing at the time was shortage of officers resulting from budget cuts. So far, to be sure, the investigation into Jack Hooper's death had not been much affected by this—perhaps because the chief superintendent did his best to protect it and perhaps even because a certain culture within the system said that all things must give way to a murder enquiry. Even Tom Foss, often inclined to complain about competing pressures on him from every direction, had produced a couple of amazingly speedy results.

But that, surely, could not go on indefinitely?

It didn't.

A spate of robberies in and around Budleigh Salterton

demanded attention. Cecilia was obliged to despatch DI Verity Jones to head up an investigation.

Thefts of equipment from farms in North Devon and Cornwall looked like the work of gangs from London. DCs Tom Wilkins and Headley Jarman must be despatched to look into those and give what help they could to overstretched local uniform.

To make matters worse, for the next few days a team from Exeter uniform had to be away at Barnstaple, assisting in duties connected with a royal visit that was scheduled for Saturday and Sunday.

All of which left Cecilia alone to continue working the case that had occupied so much of their attention over the last week or so.

"Bugger it," she muttered to herself (an expression she appeared to have picked up from junior officers and still hoped she would manage not to use in front of the children or her mama). "And bugger those cuts!"

Mrs Walker came in to see the body of her son that afternoon. Her daughter Aletheia and their pastor accompanied her.

If Cecilia had been expecting an outburst of grief, she was again mistaken. The two women gazed calmly and even, as it appeared, impassively on the body of their kinsman. Each in turn bent to kiss the hideously disfigured face. Their pastor said a prayer. At their request, the two women were left alone for a few minutes with the body.

Cecilia and Verity were present and so, briefly, was Glyn Davies, who afterwards spoke quietly to the mourners. Cecilia couldn't hear what he said, but Leoma Walker nodded in what seemed to be thanks and for a moment clasped his hand.

It had been a scene of quiet dignity and even, in a strange way, of beauty, the two women's evident love transfiguring what lay before them.

But then, as Joseph said to Cecilia afterwards, "Bear in mind that over the years black women have got rather used to receiving the bodies of their loved ones after they have been broken by white men."

Later that day there was a message from the chief superintendent on Cecilia's phone. "Make sure my office knows when the funeral is. Naturally I plan to attend if I can. In any case we'll be sending flowers."

FIFTY-ONE

Exeter. St Mary's Rectory. Saturday morning.

"So we're shorthanded *just* when things are starting to open up a bit and we need to get moving!" Cecilia said to Michael as they sat with the children sharing early coffee the next morning.

"And," she added, "if any pious person says, 'such things are sent to try us' I may just kill them."

"I don't see how that would help," Michael said. "Someone would have to arrest *you* and then you'd all be even more short-handed!"

She threw her napkin at him and Rosina had a fit of the giggles.

But at least she managed not to use the "b" word.

Putting her frustrations aside as best she could, Cecilia started work soon after she arrived at the Heavitree Station with a video conversation arranged for her by Joseph. It was with the Swiss investigator who had overseen the enquiry into the fire that had killed almost the entire Saunders' family. As it happened, they had been staying at a small villa near Bellinzona in Ticino, the Italian-speaking canton of Switzerland. So, though the Swiss Italian—*svizzero italiano*—of the investigator with whom Cecilia spoke was hardly what she had been brought up to regard as correct Italian, still, they were perfectly well able to understand each other.

The fire had happened seventeen or so years ago, but clearly the investigator was still affected by what he had seen and learned in the days following it, and she respected him the more for it.

"That beautiful family," he said, "they were all in their beds and must have been sleeping and were caught quite unawares. The place was old and it went up like kindling. There was nothing the fire service could do. They were there in minutes, but they could save no one."

Cecilia nodded.

"And you believe the fire was arson?"

"There is absolutely no doubt of it, I assure you. When we analysed the debris, it was clear that the entire lower part of the building had been drenched in accelerants: petrol and an amount of kerosene—a vicious mix, because the kerosene exploded. It was also perfectly clear where the fire had been started. I can send you the photographs, if you wish."

"Thank you, I should appreciate that. And you have no clue as to motive?"

"No, nor as to the identity of the arsonist. All the bodies of members of the family were identified—save of course Charles Saunders, who got out—and there was one additional body that we cannot identify. It was horribly burned, and a petrol can was beside it. Our surmise is that it was the arsonist himself, unwittingly caught in the fire that he had set. One might say, he was taken in his own wickedness. Having created and surrounded himself with so much that was flammable, it would have been an easy mistake to make." He paused for a moment and then concluded, "But fatal."

Again Cecilia nodded.

"The family member," she said, "the one who escaped the fire—

Charles Saunders—did he say anything about why he was so lucky when his family weren't?"

"Of course he was terribly shaken—traumatized—and also had serious burns around his head and face, so he by no means got out scot free. He was lucky not to lose his sight."

"I see."

"When the fire broke out he had just got out of bed and gone to a bathroom to relieve himself. So he was in the one room in the house were there was a possibility of survival. That is how he managed to live when everyone else in his family died."

"So it didn't occur to you that the family member who escaped—Charles Saunders himself—might have been the arsonist?"

"Certainly that possibility did occur to us. But we went carefully into the relationships of the family, including checking with people who knew them in England and had known them for years. All the evidence was that as a family they were happy and united—a functional family in every way. No sign of smouldering hatreds or desire for monetary gain. There was no reason that we could see for Charles Saunders to have murdered his family in cold blood, and no evidence that he had."

"I see. Thank you." She paused. "Did you by any chance check the DNA of the various family members who had died?"

"It wasn't necessary. They were not so badly burned as to be unrecognizable. They were all identified by Charles Saunders himself."

"I see. And did you check the DNA of the unknown person who perished?"

"We did. It corresponded to no one on any data base to which we had access."

"Do you think that when you send me the photographs of the debris, you could also send me a sample of the unknown person's DNA?"

"Of course."

FIFTY-TWO

Exeter, Heavitree Police Station, in what Joseph calls "the Boffins' Underground Kingdom." Later that morning.

"Verity tells me," Cecilia said to Joseph, "that you looked up Charles Saunders' surviving relatives. And it turns out that there's a grandmother on his father's side at a care home for the elderly in Dorset?"

"That's right," Joseph said.

"And apparently she's suffering from dementia?"

"I'm afraid so."

"How do we know that?"

"I think the family made an announcement in the papers—some years ago, actually. But let me check."

He peered at his computer and searched for some minutes, and finally said, "Yes, that's right. There was an announcement expressing deep sorrow and regret, and described as being 'by the family.' It appeared in a couple of local newspapers."

"And that was all?"

"So far as I can see. I'm not finding anything else."

"But isn't that a bit odd?—that a family member would write a notice in a newspaper saying another family member had dementia? I've never seen such a notice. At least, not about someone still alive. Have you?"

Joseph pursed his lips and shook his head. "I can't think of any. But I suppose it might be a way of protecting them from the world. 'Don't go bothering our poor relative, because he or she can't deal with it.'"

"It might. But in that case, with a family like the Saunders, wouldn't you have expected something a bit more prestigious than a couple of locals? Say, The Times and The Telegraph?"

He pursed his lips and nodded slowly.

"Yes," he said, "I think perhaps you would."

"And when exactly were these announcements published?"

He checked.

"Both in the same week—same day, actually—Thursday the 17th of May, 2003."

"At which point 'the family' was already in effect Charles Saunders, since everyone else was dead."

"That's true."

He gazed at her.

"And of course," he said slowly, "one reason why you might avoid papers like The Times and The Telegraph is that they would in fact check very carefully before publishing such a notice as this. Small local papers—perhaps not so much."

She nodded.

"That's exactly what I was thinking. Do you have a name and present address for this lady?"

"I'm sure we can find one."

Joseph peered at his computer, typed something in, then nodded and wrote on a piece of paper, which he handed to Cecilia.

She looked at it and smiled.

"Mrs Sarah Delacroix, at Bimport. That's not far. I could be there and back in a couple of hours. I think I might just pay Sarah Delacroix a visit. It would be interesting to know just how serious is her dementia, and what, if anything, she knows or thinks she knows about her grandson."

FIFTY-THREE

Bimport in Dorset. Later the same day.

Since all the other members of the Serious Crimes Team occupied elsewhere, Cecilia took PC Brenda Cosgrove with her to Bimport.

"Wear plain clothes," she said. "We don't want to frighten the poor old thing to death."

They arrived at the care home—a pleasant building amid large gardens that looked once to have been a private house—in the early afternoon. They introduced themselves first to the manager, a plump, pleasant, sensible-seeming woman who, perhaps not entirely to Cecilia's surprise, was more than somewhat dismissive of the "dementia" notice.

"I really can't imagine what led the family to do that," she said. "Even now—well, it's true she's getting a bit absent minded and forgetful—so am I! And she's fragile—as she's entitled to be: she's ninety-five! Even so, she still functions perfectly well, so far as I can see, and is one of our easiest to care for. She's always on time for meals, and she's got a good sense of humour! Her only problem is she's a bit lonely. That grandson of hers is her only surviving relative. He felt free to post notices about her having dementia all those years ago but the fact is he hasn't been to see her once in all the years since the tragedy."

"Really?"

"Never once. And she likes having visitors. So she'll be glad to see you."

Sarah Delacroix when they met with her was all that the manager said: beautifully groomed and dressed, gracious and quick. She offered them tea, which they accepted and which she proceeded to make, so far as Cecilia could see, perfectly efficiently.

Of course she'd been devastated by the family tragedy in Switzerland, and saddened by the fact that her grandson Charles, with whom she thought she had always got on quite well, had never been to see her since. She gave him the benefit of the doubt, however, suggesting it had to be the trauma of the awful thing that had happened that had led to this behaviour.

"He was always a kind boy," she said, as they were sitting with their cups of tea, "but I suppose that with my son and his dear mother and sister all gone, Charles just can't bear to see *anyone* he knew before. His old form master, Mr Hawke-Genn, has been to see me a number of times. And I know he is very sad that Charles now never returns to the college or has anything to do with any of us. But I imagine we all just bring back to the dear boy all that he has lost in a way that's too much for him to endure. Anyway, I keep him in my prayers, so we aren't totally cut off from each other, even if he doesn't know that."

After they had chatted for some time, Cecilia said, "Mrs Delacroix, do you know what DNA is?"

"Of course, dear. It's a molecule that contains our individual genetic coding. I believe it's very valuable for identifying people in your kind of work."

So much for senile dementia!

With some trepidation, Cecilia now made her key request.

"Mrs Delacroix, I fear that there are still some mysteries

surrounding the death of your family. It's possible that a sample of DNA from a family member might help get us unlock them. Would you be willing to give us such a sample?"

"Of course I would, dear. After all, nothing could be easier, could it? And if there are still mysteries surrounding what happened, I'd like to see them unravelled."

Well, that was easy enough.

"If that woman is suffering from dementia," Brenda Cosgrove said as they were driving away, "then I hope I get it too when I'm old!"

"I agree with you. She's sharp as a tack."

They drove on for a few minutes.

"So how did you like being an acting detective this morning?" Cecilia said.

"I loved it," Brenda said. "People talk to you in a way they don't when you're wearing the uniform, don't they?"

"I think that's often true," Cecilia said, "but not always. Sometimes people actually find the sight of the uniform re-assuring. It all depends on the situation. Michael says the same thing goes for clerical collars. Sometimes people are more relaxed when he's not dressed as a priest, at other times it seems important that he is."

There was a pause.

"Anyway," she said, "you certainly put Mrs Delacroix at ease—especially when you asked her about the photographs of her dogs. Well done!"

Brenda laughed. "That wasn't difficult. I love dogs and I always find other people's dogs interesting."

"And that's why you were so effective," Cecilia said. "You were *really* interested. I think that on some level people always know when we're faking it."

After a few minutes she said, "Have you ever thought about applying for detective?"

"A bit. Bob says he reckons I'd be a good detective. But he knows I also love working with the dogs."

Cecilia nodded.

"Well," she said, "that's important too. And everyone says you're marvellous at it. Not least among them my husband."

As she said this, she shook her head at the reminiscence, recalling—emotion recollected in tranquillity—a certain terrible night when she had been shot and PC Brenda had, so she had learnt from Michael and others afterward, been brilliant with a near hysterical Figaro.

FIFTY-FOUR

Exeter, Heavitree Police Station. Late that afternoon.

When they arrived back at Heavitree, there was a piece of good news. Robert Cornellissen had turned up, alive and well, and totally taken aback to find that he was a "missing person". Apparently this model among youthful merchant bankers had suddenly lost his cool and gone off for a mad and passionate few days with a young woman he met at a party.

"Lucky girl!" was all PC Annwn had to say when she heard the story.

Fortunately the bank thought well enough of young Cornellissen not to fire him, and by all accounts the young woman was neither dissatisfied with her week nor especially put out when she discovered that it had been the subject of a police investigation. So no harm seemed to have been done. It would surely have been well if he had attempted to telephone his mother rather sooner, or at least troubled to notice that the battery of his iPhone was completely dead so that neither his mother nor anyone else could call him. But he had broken no laws, and beyond youthful passion and a degree of absent-mindedness in the matter of his phone—and he had surely not been expecting his mother to call him at his work or anywhere else nearly so soon as she did—there seemed little for which to blame him.

Did he know one Armand Gagnon, a young man who had caused much confusion by pretending to be him?

Yes, he did—slightly, as an occasional drinking companion in some of the more fashionable pubs around Chelsea. Why? Did it matter?

Well, it mattered in that it suggested that Armand Gagnon, habitual liar and deceiver, knew young Cornellissen well enough to be aware that he hailed from Topsham, that his mother still lived there in something called Ambrose House, and even that she was called Letitia. So Robert Cornellissen was Armand's natural and instant choice for a fake identity when, having been phoned by his brother on his mobile and summoned to give him assistance, he found himself on a quay in Topsham by the boat where said brother was hiding out, and was challenged by the police.

Of course the fake identity if investigated would have been exposed as fake within minutes, and of course the intended assistance turned out to be no assistance at all. If he'd been resourceful enough he might at least have provided a distraction while his brother escaped. But in the event he did not even manage that, and the brother had to escape for himself.

But that was pretty well par for the course in one whose entire career was a failure, ending with a feeble attempt to blackmail the man who had employed his brother in a little matter of murder, and two small bullets in his heart.

"But wait a minute," Verity said after hearing all this. "Weren't there *two* young men on the quay that night? So what happened to the other one?"

"Good question," Cecilia said. "And I don't know."

FIFTY-FIVE

Heavitree Police Station, Cecilia's office.
Monday 1st October.

Cecilia looked at the photographs of charred remnants that the Swiss investigator emailed to her, had them printed off, then took them and showed them to a fire prevention officer who happened to be a member of the St Mary's congregation.

He looked at them and shook his head.

"Your Swiss friends knew their business," he said, arranging them on the table and then peering at them again. "They were right. That fire was started deliberately. I admit the photographs tell you nothing as to *who* started it, but there's no doubt as to the *how*. That's arson if I ever saw it."

"Right. Thank you."

Quite why she'd done this double check she wasn't entirely sure, but there'd been no harm in getting a second opinion. And in any case she certainly wasn't dissatisfied with the result.

"I think," she said to the Chief Superintendent an hour or so later, "that I may have the beginnings of an idea. But I need to test it. Is there any way we can get our hands on a sample of Charles Saunders' DNA?"

His eyebrows shot up. It was a strange request, but he trusted her.

"I'll talk to Sir Bernard," he said.

"MI5 will certainly have his DNA on file," Sir Bernard said when told of this request via Glyn Davies' secure line half an hour or so later, "so I dare say I can get it for you. But you know you won't be able to use it in court, don't you? It won't stand up. Not if you've obtained it without his permission and without a warrant."

"I don't think Cecilia cares at the moment whether it will stand up or not," Glyn Davies said. "I think she's got a theory and she's just trying to find out whether she might be thinking along the right lines."

"All right," Sir Bernard said. "I'll see what I can do."

FIFTY-SIX

Sir Bernard was as good as—or perhaps one should say better than—his word.

A package arrived by special messenger at the Chief Superintendent's office on the Wednesday afternoon. It contained a test tube with a bit of cotton wool in it, and a printed note containing six words and a name.

> *This is what you asked for.*
> *Bernard*

Glyn Davies gave a whimsical little smile as he put the tube and the note carefully back into their package.

Some minutes later he knocked and at Cecilia's call entered her office. She was sitting frowning at her computer, and looked up at him with evident surprise as he laid the package on her desk.

"A present for you from London," he said.

"Now who on earth—?"

He raised a finger to his lips and shook his head.

She stopped.

"As I say, a present for you from London"—with which he turned on his heel and left.

Cecilia unpacked her "present", looked at it for a few minutes, read the note, then smiled and nodded and picked up her telephone.

"Tom," she said when she was through to forensics, "I've got something for you."

Tom Foss had one of his team over to Cecilia's office to collect her 'present' within the hour.

"Dr Foss will have the lab compare it as soon as possible," the young woman said brightly. But then came the downer. "I think we should know the result in a week. Not more than two, anyway."

"A week?" Cecilia said to her. "This really is rather urgent. Couldn't we do better than that?"

"I doubt it, ma'am. They're short handed and way behind."

Cecilia groaned mentally. It was the usual story. And what if their suspect disappeared before they got their result? — Something that, if her suspicions were right, he was really rather good at.

But then on the following day, which was a Wednesday, Tom Foss himself called her midmorning.

"I've got your result," he said.

"*Already?* But I thought it would take a week. How on earth—?"

"You really don't want to know. Let's just say you owe me."

"Oh. All right then! I owe you."

"But here's what you *do* want to know. It's identical."

She narrowly suppressed a whoop.

"Thank you, Tom," she said. "You've just made me a very happy woman."

"Good," he said. "What else do I live for?"

She replaced the handset and sat for a while, gazing into space.

"Gotcha!" she said finally.

Fifty-Seven

Heavitree Police Station. The office of the Chief Superintendent.
Mid-afternoon on Wednesday 3rd October

"Now let me be clear," Glyn Davies said. "What we've actually got that we can use in court is one piece of hearsay evidence that would be admissible since the original witness is dead—?"

"Yes," Cecilia said. "I've put some feelers out. Obviously there *were* other witnesses. And first-hand would be better. But no luck so far."

"And there may well not be. It *was* twenty-three years ago. But the other thing we have that convinces you that Saunders is your man is the DNA?"

"Yes, sir. Tom Foss has double-checked everything, and he's sure it's identical. And that clinches it. The man in MI5 who calls himself Saunders *is* the man who held Gladstone Walker by the collar twenty-three years ago when Walker was shot in the head."

"Which is fine except that the DNA evidence was obtained in such a way that you won't be able to use it in court—correct? But once we arrest him, then we'll be entitled to insist on a DNA sample from him that we *can* use."

"Yes, sir. And once we've arrested him we can also search his premises. That might turn up all sorts of stuff."

"Indeed it might." Glyn Davies looked at her wryly. "Or of course it might not." He paused. "I'll tell you now, CPR don't like this one bit—and I generally take what they say seriously because at the end of the day they're the ones who get landed with having to argue it in court. They're worried that if the evidence doesn't work out as you expect—if for some reason there's been a mistake and Saunders' own DNA when we get it actually *isn't* a match for whoever held on to Gladstone Walker twenty-three years ago—then we'll end up with a great deal of egg on our faces and most likely a massive suit for wrongful arrest."

Cecilia was about to assure him of her confidence in Tom Foss's work, but before she could speak he gave her a half-smile and continued, "Nevertheless, it *is* my decision, not CPR's. And I trust you and Tom Foss. If you are right, this is an extremely dangerous man who can't be off the streets soon enough. So I'm going to risk it. I'll apply for a warrant to arrest Saunders on 'the basis of information received.'"

She nodded. To obtain a warrant for the arrest they wouldn't be obliged actually to *produce* their evidence, merely name the suspect and the alleged offence. The problem, if there was one, would arise twenty-four hours after the arrest when they'd be obliged to bring the suspect into court before a magistrate and there produce at least enough evidence to establish a prima facie case against him. Given the little they had, this was indeed a risk, and in asking for the warrant Glyn Davies would be putting himself on the line as much as her.

"Thank you, sir," she said. "I do appreciate this. I'm afraid there are a lot of ifs."

He chuckled and shook his head. "We live in an age of uncertainty."

Another thought occurred to her. "One question of protocol, sir. Do I have enough rank to arrest someone in MI5?"

He seemed if anything amused at her question.

"Of course you do," he said. "Actually, an MI5 agent as such has no rank at all. So if it comes to that, even a police constable can arrest him, let alone a mighty superintendent of detectives."

Of course this was serious business, but Cecilia found herself giggling. So far as she could recall, no one had ever called her "mighty" before.

Glyn Davies, however, was now entering into the spirit of the thing and in full flow.

"If, however, you're bent on doing the terrible deed inside Thames House rather than on the street in Millbank—and I rather gather you are—we'll need to get permission. Ordinary coppers such as you and me aren't usually allowed into Thames House. Too many secrets! Anyway, leave that side of things to me. I'll call you later."

Glyn Davies was again as good as his word.

He phoned her that evening at home.

"You need to be here in the morning at eight," he said. "There'll be a car to pick us up. I'd go on the train but they're so damned unreliable these days and I don't want anything to go wrong. Sir Bernard knows we're coming and we'll be admitted as soon as we arrive. Once we've made the arrest, of course we'll have a right to search the fellow's premises. All we'll need for that is an instruction from one of us. I'll take care of that. Sir Bernard's arranging for officers from the Met to help with the search, and as all your team are busy I've arranged with Bob Coulter to come with us tomorrow to head it up." He paused. "As you'll have gathered, I'm planning to come with you."

She smiled. She'd worked with Glyn Davies quite long enough to know he wasn't the man to miss out on a bit of excitement away from his desk—and after all he'd done to make this particular piece of excitement happen he surely deserved it. It also meant, of course, that as the senior officer involved he would be firmly in the firing line if anything went wrong.

"When we arrive," he continued, "I'm going to come into Thames House with you but I still want you to make the actual arrest. It's your case, so that's only right. As it's on the Met's patch, when we arrive at Thames House we'll be joined at the entrance by a couple of their officers who'll also come in with us, but they'll simply be there to assist. And after you've made the arrest the Met's providing a van that'll bring the prisoner back to Exeter for us."

He paused. "I think that's all. Can you think of anything else?"

"No, sir, I can't. Thank you."

"Oh, wait a minute," he said. "There *is* one other thing. Cecilia, Sir Bernard says to wear your uniform. Let the blighter see it's all official and we aren't messing about. Apart from that, you handle the questioning and the arrest just as you like. I'll be there to look benevolent… or maybe fierce? A fierce minion of the law? Olwen and Arwen say I'm quite good at looking fierce. But whatever you think is appropriate."

Cecilia laughed.

"Oh, definitely fierce, sir. We all find your fierceness *extremely* terrifying, so I'm sure Saunders will."

Michael would, of course, make gleeful and somewhat salacious remarks when he saw her putting on her uniform. He always said he specially fancied her in that.

FIFTY-EIGHT

Millbank, London SW1.
Thursday, 4th October

They arrived at Thames House exactly on schedule. A Metropolitan Police van and a police car were already parked in Millbank, and two uniformed Metropolitan police officers, a sergeant and a constable, met them as arranged under the massive arch that spans the entry. After a minimum of introduction the group made its way through the triple doors to be greeted immediately by two young men in dark, single-breasted suits, one of whom said, "Good morning gentlemen, ma'am. Sir Bernard told us to expect you. This way, please." The two then set off, leaving the police officers to follow.

It was a vast building, but surprisingly quiet, the chief sound, it seemed to Cecilia, being their own shoes on the marble floors. For some time they were making their way along long and lofty corridors—surely corridors of power!—with many doors. A seemingly endless succession of oil-painted worthies from previous centuries gazed down upon them as they passed, with an occasional marble bust for variety. If you were especially important did you get a marble bust as well as a painting?

At one point an elderly man with a silver topped walking stick appeared for a moment by one of the doors. He gave a faint smile and nod to Glyn Davies, who nodded back. He gave an even fainter smile and nod to Cecilia and the rest of the party, and then disappeared back through the doorway. He was, Cecilia suspected, the great Sir Bernard Hough, without whose fiat none of this would be happening.

The young men who were leading the way eventually stopped by another lofty door, identical to all the others, so far as she could see—save that she now noted a small brass plaque with "Saunders" on it in black letters.

"This is it," one of them said.

"Thank you," the Chief Superintendent said. "We can manage from here. Just follow us in."

He knocked on the door and entered without waiting for an answer.

Cecilia and Bob Coulter and the two Metropolitan officers followed him, trailed by the dark-suited young men.

The room was exactly as the officer from Counter Terrorism had described it: spacious, with a large mahogany desk in the middle on which there reposed an elegant Victorian silver inkstand.

The man behind the desk looked up: small, dapper and balding, immaculate in a charcoal suit and old Etonian tie.

"What the devil—?" he began and then, evidently registering their uniforms, "For heaven's sake, haven't you people *yet* wasted enough of your own time and tax-payers money? Not to mention wasting *my* time, which I dare say is more valuable than any of yours."

Of course he addressed the Chief Superintendent, the man in charge.

Glyn Davies, however, merely looked at Cecilia, who stepped forward.

"You are Charles Edward Saunders?" she said formally.

"You all know damned well who I am," he said, momentarily switching his regard to her. "And I can scarcely believe," he continued, turning his address back to the Chief Superintendent, "that you people are still intending to pursue this farce about documents that you clearly do not understand, even though they've been explained to you in terms that a five-year-old ought to be able to grasp. You may be quite sure I shall be taking all this up with the commissioner."

Ignoring all this, Cecilia now walked right up to his desk, lent over it and shoved the Victorian silver inkstand aside, scattering papers that lay behind it and leaving it so that it lay awkwardly and untidily askew. Having thus regained his outraged attention—

"Charles Edward Saunders," she said quietly, "alias William Craig, I am arresting you for the murder of Gladstone Stewart Walker close by Winterbourne Woods near Exeter in the County of Devon on the second of June 1994. You do not have to say anything. But it may harm your defence if you do not mention when questioned something which you later rely on in Court. Anything you do say may be given in evidence."

"How *dare* you—!"

"Do you understand?"

"I understand this is a bloody impertinence."

She nodded. His words were aggressive and he had risen to his feet. But at least he was now addressing her.

"I'll take that as a 'yes'," she said. "Constable, handcuff this man for me, will you."

"Yes ma'am," said the constable, and produced a set of handcuffs.

Cecilia continued as the constable was carrying out her task, "Since you are being arrested for an offence committed in Exeter, you will now be taken to Exeter to be interviewed and to answer charges before a magistrate there. You will of course be entitled to legal counsel. I shall also be requiring a DNA sample from you."

Out of the corner of her eye, she noticed as Glyn Davies passed a folded paper to Bob Coulter, who took it, nodded, and promptly left, accompanied by one of the dark-suited young men.

Saunders-alias-Craig was protesting.

"This is outrageous. I most certainly will not give you a DNA sample and you have no right to ask for it—"

"On the contrary Mr Saunders, since you've just been arrested and charged with a recordable offence and the sample I require is in connection with that offence, I have every right. What's more, if you refuse to comply, the officers may use reasonable force to obtain it. Constable, will you take Mr Saunders to his transport?"

"Ma'am."

FIFTY-NINE

Saunders's apartment in Westminster, about fifteen minutes later.

As had been arranged, Bob Coulter rendezvoused with four officers from the Met at the entrance to Saunders's apartment, bringing with him authority from Chief Superintendent Davies to enter and search it.

If the young constables—two male, two female—had imagined their colleague from the west country would be slow on the uptake or need guidance from his smart London team, they were soon disabused. The wiry ex-soldier, himself a Londoner by birth, took charge effortlessly and directed their search with skill and precision, wasting no time, but making sure they omitted nothing.

As the constables went about their task, Bob Coulter gazed speculatively at the ostentatious opulence that surrounded them: the television that covered most of one wall in one of the reception rooms, the vast stereo, the luxury bathroom with gold-plated fittings. Once he would have coveted such toys. But then his years in the army had taught him that some things were more important than toys—things such as good mates who stuck by you under fire. And his last eighteen months or so with Brenda had taught him something more. It would've been hard for him to describe it: a warm blur of comfortable, threadbare furniture and a generous kitchen, of egg and chips and cups of tea, of dogs—dogs of every shape and size!—and Brenda's kisses and going with her to see Father Michael and above all knowing he was happy when he was with her in a way that no one and nothing had ever made him happy before.

So the expensive toys, once duly noted, moved him if at all merely to amusement as he focussed rapidly—the army had taught him that too!—on the job in hand: finding possible hiding places. They must leave nothing unchecked. The major (he still thought of Glyn Davies by the army rank in which he had first known him) was depending on it.

Ten minutes or so later—

"Sergeant!" came a voice from the master bedroom. "I think I've got something you might want to look at."

The constable was standing by a chest of drawers. The top drawer was open.

"I was going through and I wondered about those," she said and pointed.

The drawer contained several pairs of gloves, neatly laid out. Most of them appeared as new, but one pair had a slightly battered appearance.

"I just thought those looked a bit out of place," she said. "All the other pairs look like they're on a counter in a posh shop."

He peered at the gloves and nodded. "You're right," he said. "Well spotted. Photograph them and then bag them for evidence. They could be very interesting."

"Whoa! Here's something else!" another constable said, looking up from where he was kneeling by the enormous bed. He reached under it and pulled, and by the time Bob Coulter was at his side he had it out.

It was "something" indeed: a slim, beautifully polished mahogany box with brass fittings and a brass key protruding from the lock. They photographed it.

"Shall I open it, sergeant?"

"Go for it!"

The key turned easily and the box opened to reveal green velvet lining in which were set a tiny, gleaming pistol, a cartridge box and a cleaner.

Bob Coulter smiled. He'd never actually seen one before, but he'd seen plenty of pictures and even if the name hadn't been engraved on the grip he'd have known exactly what he was looking at: an immaculate specimen of the 2.7mm semi-automatic pistol known as Kolibri.

"It's hardly big enough to get hold of," the constable said. "Is it a real gun? Will it fire?"

"Oh, it's real all right," Bob Coulter said. "And unless I'm very much mistaken it's been used to kill at least two people already."

SIXTY

Exeter, at about the same time.

"Weren't there two young men on the quay that night?" Verity had said some days ago. "So what happened to the other one?"

What indeed?

Using descriptions provided by PCs Merchant and Lloyd, uniformed officers had made enquiries in the neighbourhood over the next couple of days. And the enquiries bore fruit. It turned out that the landlord of the Kings Head, just off Topsham Quay, knew just such a young man as they described. Actually, he knew him quite well.

"A harmless enough lad, so far as I can see. Bill Suggs he's called, and he's at the university. I think he's doing something called Business and Management."

"And he was here on the fourth?"

"He was. It wasn't like normal, though. Usually he comes in with a group of his mates, more or less the same lot every time, undergrads like him. This time he was alone—and already a bit the worse for wear."

Suggs had then palled up in the bar with a young fellow the

landlord didn't know, but who from the landlord's description was surely Armand Gagnon. The pair of them sat drinking in the corner of the bar until about eleven, and then departed in an alcoholic haze of good fellowship after, as the landlord put it, "I told them straight, 'You two have had enough. Time to go home!'"

On the basis of all this, it hadn't been difficult to find Bill Suggs himself. Sergeant Stillwell and a constable approached him on the University campus on Thursday morning as he was on his way to a lecture.

"We have information," Sergeant Stillwell said, "that in an apparently inebriated state you approached two police officers on Topsham Quay on the night of fourth of September."

"Oh my God, yes. I was drunk out of my mind. I'm sorry officer. Am I in trouble?"

"It's not up to us to say, sir. But as a result of what happened you are now of interest in an ongoing murder investigation."

"*Murder*? That's ridiculous. That business on the quay—that was just a bit of fun!"

"That's as may be, sir. I'm afraid our colleagues don't have much sense of humour when it's a murder case."

"But—"

"So, sir, this can go one of two ways. Either we can arrest you now on suspicion of conspiracy to pervert the cause of justice. Or you need to come down voluntarily to Heavitree Police Station and assist us in our enquiries. Your choice."

"Oh my God. Of course I'll come."

"Good. Is that a mobile phone you've got there?"

"Yes."

"Show me the number."

Bill Suggs did as he was told.

"Right," Stillwell said. "Now here's what'll happen. Some time in the next twenty-four hours you'll get a phone call or a text from us telling you when you're wanted for interview. So keep your phone on and keep it charged and answer it whenever you get a call from Devon and Cornwall Police. Whatever time they tell you, cancel whatever else you think you have on and be there. And be on time. Or I promise you my lad there'll be a warrant out for your arrest quicker than you can say Jack Robinson."

SIXTY-ONE

An interview room at Heavitree Police Station.
The following morning: Friday, 5th September.

Facing Cecilia across the table would be Charles Saunders, already seated when she arrived and looking none-the-worse for his night in the cells, and seated beside him a solicitor, Roy Charles John Gillon, a local man with offices in the Cathedral Close.

Cecilia gave a half-smile and nodded in greeting to Gillon as she took her seat. He gave a similar slight smile and nodded back. She'd crossed swords with him before, and respected him. He was a somewhat severe, formal man, perhaps not overly gifted with a sense of humour. But he knew his job, and had on occasion stopped her full in her tracks. On the other hand, she had the sense that he respected her as an officer not inclined to cheat with the evidence, and willing when appropriate to allow those in custody the benefit of the doubt.

All that granted, Cecilia was in fact feeling fairly confident. She had two new pieces of evidence, one that she had not possessed before this morning in a form that she could use in court, the other entirely fresh. ·

Other detectives in the Serious Crime Team were still all busy elsewhere—Verity with her spate of burglaries, and Tom and Headley with their criminal gangs. So Cecilia had with her for the interview Bob Coulter.

The Chief Superintendent and Joseph would be watching from outside through the two-way mirror. Sergeant Stilwell, the rugby player, was standing by the door.

She began, as was her custom, by pointing out that the interview was being video-recorded, and that this recording was as much for the benefit of the person in custody as for the benefit of the police.

She continued, "In this interview I shall be putting various questions to you. You were told when you were arrested that you did not have to say anything. That is still the case. You don't have to answer my questions or co-operate with me in any way at all."

"Do you think I don't already know all this?" Saunders said testily.

"It's of no concern to me whether you know it already or not. My concern is to make sure that you are informed of your rights *now*. Your legal counsel will no doubt advise you on when and how and whether to co-operate with me, and I dare say you will be wise to follow his advice, which in my experience is invariably good."

Mr Gillon the solicitor raised an eyebrow, but said nothing.

"Now, Charles Edward Saunders, also known as William Craig, you are charged in the first instance with the murder of Gladstone Walker in 1994. Do you have anything to say?"

Saunders looked at his solicitor.

Gillon said, "You make two assertions: first that my client Charles Saunders is in fact one William Craig who disappeared some years ago; and second, that William Craig murdered Gladstone Walker. I take it the police have evidence for both these assertions?"

"We do. First, and most important,"—she now turned back to Saunders—"your DNA, known to us by the DNA sample obtained from you yesterday, is identical with the DNA of Gladstone Walker's assailant."

"And we are to understand," Gillon said, "that the police are sure about the DNA of Gladstone Walker's assailant twenty-three years ago?"

"We are, Mr Gillon. Under the right circumstances, as I am sure you are aware, DNA evidence lasts for a very long time. Our forensics laboratory will, of course, furnish scientific reasons for their conclusion to officers of the court and counsel for the defence at the proper time, but we are confident that it is sound."

"I see." Gillon made another note.

"Second,"—she again turned back to the man in custody—"we have witnesses who can testify that the murderer of Gladstone Walker was identified by one present at the scene as William Craig, who was quite well known to them as their political leader."

"That will then be hearsay evidence?" Mr Gillon said.

"It will, but admissible as first hand hearsay evidence, since the actual witness is dead."

Mr Gillon raised an eyebrow and then made another note. When he had finished, he looked up.

"There is, however," Cecilia said, again looking at the man in custody, "something else linking you to the death of Gladstone Walker. Would you talk to us about the gun, Sergeant Coulter?"

Bob Coulter nodded. "Gladstone Walker was killed by a bullet to the head fired point-blank from a rather unusual pistol—a 2.7mm semi-automatic manufactured in 1914, often known as the Kolibri. We have the bullet, which was still lodged in the victim's skull when Walker's body was found on the 3rd May this year. A search of Mr Saunders' apartment in London yesterday revealed—"

"I take it," Gillon said, "that the police had a warrant for this search of my client's home?"

"The search," Cecilia said, "was carried out *after* your client had been arrested and charged. We'd reason to suppose we'd find evidence in his home relating to the crime with which he was charged. As you will be aware, in such a circumstance the only authorization required for the search was from a senior officer. Sergeant Coulter, who himself headed up the search, had such authorization from Chief Superintendent Davies. We can provide you with a copy of that, too, of course."

Gillon made another note.

Cecilia indicated that Bob Coulter should continue.

"Searching Saunders' flat," he said, "we came across a Kolibri 2.7 mm semi-automatic pistol. Ballistics testing shows that it is in fact the *same* gun that was used in the execution style killing of Gladstone Walker in 1994."

Cecilia took up the story.

"We therefore conclude that William Craig as he was known then and the person known for the last several years as Charles Saunders are the same man—namely, you."

Gillon raised an eyebrow and glanced sideways at his client, who neither said anything nor looked at him.

"In connection with this," Cecilia added, "I should tell you that we have compared your DNA with a sample of DNA provided for us, with her permission, by Mrs Sarah Delacroix, at present living in Dorset. Mrs Delacroix would be your maternal grandmother if you were who you've claimed to be for the last decade and a half. The comparison makes clear that you have no familial relationship to her at all. This is a matter to which I shall have reason to return."

At this Mr Gillon continued writing for several minutes. Cecilia waited until he had finished and looked up at her again.

"Now," she said, turning back to the prisoner, "you should know that we are also going to charge you with the killing of a second man, Armand Gagnon, on Exmouth beach on the night of Monday the tenth of September. This victim was killed with a bullet fired from the same Kolibri 2.7 mm. semi-automatic that we found in your flat, the gun that killed Gladstone Walker in 1994. Armand Gagnon was then buried on the beach in soft sand."

The man in custody's expression did not change.

"The victim's clothes," Cecilia continued, "had been neatly folded and left on the beach by someone wearing gloves."

She turned again to Bob Coulter. "Sergeant Coulter?"

He too addressed the man in custody directly. "During the search of your flat yesterday, we also found the gloves that had been worn by whoever folded those clothes. And DNA testing this morning shows that those gloves have been worn by you and by no one else."

Charles Saunders alias William Craig was clearly determined to show no emotion or reaction. Yet for all that, at this revelation he surely looked ever so slightly surprised. Cecilia almost smiled. It was amazing how many people—including quite clever people— seemed still to think that wearing gloves was a protection against detection. Modern forensics could of course trace gloves almost as precisely as fingerprints.

Meanwhile Bob Coulter had glanced at his notes. He looked up and added one other thing.

"There were also grains of sand in the gloves. Those grains of sand match the sand on Exmouth beach where Armand Gagnon's body was found."

Still the man in custody said nothing.

Cecilia glanced at the clock.

"The man previously calling himself Charles Saunders and now known to us as William Craig indicates that he has nothing to say. Interview terminated at 11.55 a.m." she said, and switched off the equipment."

She looked at the interviewee. "We all need a break. I will, however, wish to see you here again at two." She added, mostly because it happened to be true, "Sergeant Coulter has to be elsewhere this afternoon. So I'll be accompanied for the next part of my interview with you by Detective Inspector Verity Jones, who is well-acquainted with the details of this case."

Bob Coulter was scheduled to be on the firing range that afternoon with two new recruits for the Armed Response Team. Verity, however, having dealt for the moment with her spate of burglaries, would be back.

The interviewee made no response to this information.

Mr Gillon the solicitor nodded in polite acknowledgment.

And Cecilia went to lunch.

SIXTY-TWO

Heavitree Police Station. Cecilia's office about twenty minutes later.

One of the catchphrases in an over-the-top American adven-
ture series that Cecilia used to watch on television when she
was little was, "I love it when a plan comes together."

And suddenly it all seemed to be doing just that. She was in her
office where she had just finished bringing Verity up to date on the
morning's exchanges when her phone rang.

It was Glyn Davies.

"I've just had word from my counterpart in Marseilles," he said.
"Actually he's an old friend of mine: Commissaire Divisionnaire
Etienne Dubois. Anyway, he tells me Marseilles police arrested
Marcel Gagnon a couple of hours ago."

Cecilia was constantly surprised by the number of "old friends"
Glyn Davies seemed to have in unexpected places. But that aside—

"That's great news, sir," she said. "Verity's here, so I'll put you
on speakerphone."

"I gather Gagnon was arrested," Glyn Davies continued, "as
he was trying to board a plane for South America—for Costa Rica,
to be exact. In the process of charging him with various offences
committed in France, the gendarmes also let him know not only

that he'd been identified beyond reasonable doubt as the murderer of Jack Hooper in England, but also let it slip that his own little brother Armand had been murdered and that the murderer was undoubtedly the man known to him as Charles Saunders of MI5. No doubt their letting that slip was inadvertent."

Of course it was!

"Any way," he went on, "having learned this, Gagnon is beside himself with fury. He doesn't attempt to deny he killed Jack Hooper. But he can hardly wait to testify to any one who will listen that Charles Saunders paid him to do it. And while we won't get to arrest and charge Gagnon until the French have had their go at him, Etienne is clear that in the meantime we'll be able to question him and even use him as a witness."

"That's useful," Cecilia said. "I've been convinced for some time that Saunders-who-is-really-Craig was behind Jack Hooper's death. I just couldn't see how to make it stick."

"What's more," Davies added, "Gagnon says he has the evidence to prove his accusation. And Etienne, who's been round the block a few times and is judge of a witness if ever I saw one, reckons if Gagnon says he's got proof, he has."

SIXTY-THREE

Heavitree Police station, later the same day.

They had arranged for Cecilia to interview Bill Suggs at one o'clock. Verity needed to catch up on her deskwork in the hour immediately after lunch, so Cecilia took PC Annwn Merchant with her. Bill Suggs was waiting for them in an interview room, tall and skinny and scared.

Annwn Merchant identified him at once.

"So what the devil did you think you were playing at the other night on the quay?" she said.

"I'm really sorry, officer. I meant no harm. Honestly. I was drunk."

"Yes, well, we'd figured that out for ourselves."

"We've been told," Cecilia said, "that when you go out for a few beers at the King's Head you usually drink with a group of friends. But that night you were drinking alone. Why was that?"

"They'd all gone to see a film."

"You don't like films?"

"I thought my girlfriend had dumped me for my mate Charlie. He's one of our gang and he's very sporting and plays cricket for the varsity first eleven and I didn't want to be with them—not if I had to see Joan and him together."

"What do you mean, you *thought* she'd dumped you?"

"It turned out she hadn't. We're back together now."

Cecilia exchanged a glance with Annwn.

"So," she continued, "suffering from the pangs of what you thought was unrequited love, although it turns out it wasn't, you decided to go and get plastered by yourself?"

"Yes, ma'am."

Cecilia raised an eyebrow.

"So then what happened?"

He frowned.

"To be honest, I'm not sure I remember it all. There was a bloke at the bar in the King's Head. We got talking."

"Tell us about him."

"He said his name was Armand. Said he was French, though he didn't have an accent, not so far as I could tell."

"And what did you talk about?"

"Oh, girls… football… stuff. Nothing really."

She could imagine.

"But then he said he'd made a bet he'd go and chat up some police who were guarding a boat on the quay. I thought it was just a bit of fun."

"So then what happened?"

"I'm not really sure. We went to the quay and after we talked with… with you…"—he looked at Annwn—"then we goofed off." He hesitated. "I seemed to lose track of Armand after that. But then I remember I sat down by someone's garden. I must have gone to sleep. I woke up when it was getting daylight with a terrible headache and lurched along to the bus stop and got the bus back to Exeter."

"So you really thought you were just joining in some kind of jolly jape on Topsham quay?"

He shifted nervously in his chair. "I suppose so."

"Well, Mr Suggs, it's never a jolly jape to interfere with the police when they're trying to do their job."

His lip was trembling. "I'm very sorry."

"You should be. As it happens, you were on the edge of being involved with some extremely violent and dangerous people. Do you know what's happened to your new friend Armand?"

"I haven't seen him since."

"I don't expect you have. He's dead."

"What?"

"He's under a sheet in a refrigerator in the morgue with two bullet holes in him."

Bill Suggs went white. "Oh... oh my God. The officer yesterday said this was in connection with murder, but—oh my God, you don't think I did it, do you?"

"If I did, Mr Suggs, you'd be under arrest. As it is, we've checked up on you with various people who know you, and overall you seem to be a tolerably law-abiding young man. And your story is just daft enough to be true. Do you agree, Constable Merchant?"

"I do, ma'am."

"Is there anything you'd want to say to Mr Suggs beyond that?"

Annwn gazed at him.

"I'd say it's generally a bad idea going out and getting drunk, but if you *must* do it then at least do it with mates you can trust to get you home."

Bill Suggs looked even more sheepish, and Cecilia nodded.

"So what are we going to do with you?" she said.

Again Suggs shifted uncomfortably in his chair.

"If general stupidity and behaving like a complete idiot were an offence under the law, I'd charge you with that. I'm *tempted* to charge you with wasting police time—which actually *is* an offence. You can go to prison for it."

His eyes widened.

"As it is," she said, "I think you may have learned your lesson. So for this one time I'm going to dismiss you without any charge. No further action will be taken."

There was a moment of silence.

He sat staring at her like the proverbial rabbit caught in headlights.

"*That*," she said finally but not unkindly, "means you can go."

"Oh, er, right, er, thank you. Thank you *so* much!"

He scuttled out.

The two police officers just managed to suppress their laughter until they were sure he had gone.

SIXTY-FOUR

Heavitree Police Station, the same interview room at 2.00 pm.

When Cecilia arrived with Verity at the interview room later that afternoon, she was aware of two new issues that they now needed to raise with Saunders. She'd asked Verity to open the session.

After indicating as usual that the conversation was being recorded and identifying the participants, Verity said, "There are two matters that were not dealt with in your interview this morning. The first is this: in addition to the charges that DSU Cavaliere has already presented to you, we shall also be charging you with conspiracy to murder in the case of Jack Hooper, who was killed on his vessel the *Falcon* on the evening of the 24th of April. I should tell you that we have a witness to this, a well-informed witness, who is in a position to prove what he claims."

This was perhaps a little optimistic on Verity's part, but then, they both trusted Glyn Davies' assessment of his source for this information.

"Do you wish to make any comment on that charge?" Verity asked, and as usual received no response.

She looked at Cecilia, who nodded at her to continue, which she did.

"The final issue we wish to raise with you today is this. As you were told at an earlier point in these interviews, DNA sampling makes it clear that you have no biological relationship at all to the woman who would be your maternal grandmother if you were truly who you have claimed to be for the last eighteen or so years. As you were also told, DNA sampling from another source indicates that you are in fact William Craig, one time leader of the extreme right political party known as the British Union.

"Two consequences arise from this identification that we have not yet considered. First, as William Craig, you will also be charged with murder and conspiracy to murder in connection with the firebombing of the Heschel family in Stepney on the fourteenth of June, 2000. There has, of course, been a warrant out for your arrest in connection with that since the fifteenth of June of the same year.

"The second consequence takes us outside the United Kingdom. The discovery of your true identity, and the discovery that a hitherto unidentified body found at the scene of the fire that caused the Saunders deaths is in fact a member of that family— these two discoveries naturally raise fresh questions over the causes of that fire and *your* role therein. We have been exchanging relevant information about this matter with the Swiss authorities for some time. We understand they will wish to question you about it, and, depending on the results of that questioning, should you actually outlive any prison sentences imposed on you as a result of crimes with which you are being charged in the United Kingdom, I dare say they will be anxious to extradite you to Switzerland to answer charges of multiple homicides there. If things stand as they are at present, none of us can imagine any Home Secretary raising the slightest objection to this."

Still there was silence. Verity looked at Cecilia, who nodded and took up the questioning.

"I put to you the suggestion that I have already made to my Swiss colleagues in Ticino: that after the firebombing of the Heschel family in London, with a European Arrest Warrant out for you, you realized that as William Craig you were a lost man. You therefore determined to make use of your physical resemblance to Charles Saunders, as well as your intimate knowledge of Saunders family, so as to achieve a change of identity. You fired the house the Saunders were in, annihilating the entire family in an act of fourfold murder—a family, I would note, who had over many years shown you nothing but kindness and goodwill. You then impersonated their son Charles, whom you resembled, presenting yourself as the family's sole survivor.

"Of course you could only get away with this for so long as you succeeded in avoiding anyone who really knew Charles Saunders or you. So you resigned Saunders' position in the diplomatic service, pleading trauma, which was I suppose credible enough in one who alleged he was sole survivor of a terrible tragedy. Of course you never went back to see the one surviving Saunders relative, who would certainly have recognized that you were not her grandson. You chose instead to plant at large the wicked and utterly untrue notion that that bright, delightful old lady was suffering from dementia. And of course you never went back to your old school, where masters such as Francis Hawke-Genn who had once taught you would also have seen immediately through your deception. And when by mere chance you saw and recognized in the street Jack Hooper, a man who had been your follower in your British Union days, convinced that he'd recognized you and characteristically unwilling to leave any kind of loose end, you paid an assassin to kill him. That, I suggest, is essentially your story."

She paused.

Silence.

"DI Jones, do you have any further questions or comments for this man?"

"No, ma'am."

"William Craig, do you have anything that you wish to say or any questions that you wish to ask in connection with any of the charges that are being brought against you?"

He stared past her and still said nothing.

"William Craig alias Charles Saunders does not speak. Interview terminated at two-twenty p.m."

She switched off the equipment. She and Verity rose to their feet and started to leave.

"You can take all the high and mighty tone you like," Craig said, suddenly breaking his silence as they approached the door, "the fact remains, I did what I did because I am a patriot."

Cecilia turned and looked back at him.

"What did you say?"

"I am a patriot. I believe in this country, in Britain. With a name like yours, of course you wouldn't understand that. But we survived two world wars—victorious. We stood strong when the whole of Europe was against us."

She gazed at him for a moment.

"We?" she said finally. "You weren't even born."

"We the nation," he said, "we the British people. Our greatness is in our genes. *We* survived and were victorious."

"Actually," Verity said, "there were rather a lot of us *didn't* survive. Including my great granddad. He died on D-Day on a beach called Gold in Normandy. He was just married and aged twenty. He never saw his son."

Cecilia gazed at Verity in some surprise as she choked slightly on the last sentence. There were tears in her eyes.

"Of course," Craig said, "it is regrettable that your great grandfather should have lost his life. But in every great cause sacrifices must be made."

"And that's the difference," Cecilia said, "between you and DI Jones's great grandpapa. He sacrificed himself. That's what soldiers do. You sacrifice other people. That's what criminals do."

He shook his head.

"Western civilization," he said, "*white* civilization, has abandoned its calling, and the world is falling apart as a result of it. Or am I the only one that's noticed?"

There was silence.

"Mr Craig," she said finally, "allow me to offer you a reality check. Regardless of what I or anyone else may think of your political opinions, you are not under arrest because of them. You are under arrest charged with murder and conspiracy to murder, which are crimes under law—under *English* law. Good afternoon. And good afternoon to you, Mr Gillon."

At which Mr Gillon the solicitor swept his papers together and rose to his feet. Was it actually a smile that with careful professional tact he was doing his best to hide?

"And good afternoon to *you*, Detective Superintendent Cavaliere, Detective Inspector Jones," he replied.

Only William Craig remained seated, gazing sullenly down at the table in front of him. It was as if there was a black cloud over his head. Cecilia gazed back. He'd been given so much—a good education, money, culture, friends. He could have been so much. He could have given so much back. He could have done so much.

He could even have been happy.

Yet all he did was spew death.

What was wrong with such a man? What on earth made him like that?

Suddenly, surprizing even herself, she found herself pitying him.

SIXTY-FIVE

Heavitree Police Station, on the way to Cecilia's office.
A few minutes later

"I hope," Verity said as they walked back from the interview room towards Cecilia's office, "that I'm not a vindictive person. I was always brought up to try and see the best in everyone."

Cecilia raised an eyebrow. Of all the people she knew, Verity Jones was probably the least vindictive she could think of.

Verity, however, hadn't finished.

"But I must admit," she said, "I really hope that fellow Saunders or Craig or whatever he wants to call himself now has a tough time in prison."

Cecilia sighed. "If he carries on like that, he probably will. And God help him if he's sent to Belmarsh."

"What was it first put you on to Saunders being Craig?" Verity asked. "I can see it now you've put it together—but what started you?"

Cecilia thought for a moment.

"I think," she said finally, "it was hearing how meticulously tidy William Craig was when he was at school, and how untidy and chaotic Charles Saunders was. And then the anti-terrorism chaps who saw Charles Saunders described him being meticulous and fussy just the way Craig used to be. It was as if they'd swopped personalities. Then it struck me that this new and Craig-like Saunders had appeared at more or less exactly the same time as William Craig disappeared. And I started to wonder. I started wondering about that boy who was murdered on the beach—and his clothes being so neatly folded! And then the more I checked and thought about it, the more the pieces seemed to come together."

Verity nodded. "Well, I think your logic was brilliant."

Cecilia laughed. She'd long considered Verity a dear and loyal friend, but Verity did not often compliment her on her logic.

Sixty-Six

St Mary's Rectory, that evening

Cecilia would be home soon. Her mama and papa were coming to supper, and so were Verity and Joseph with Samuel. Cecilia's parents would bring their dogs Tocco and Pu, and Verity and Joseph would bring Hoover. So no doubt it would be an evening of happy chaos.

It was Michael's turn to cook. In this he was being assisted by Rachel and (at least in theory) her sister Rosina. Figaro had his usual watching brief from a dog bed near the Aga while Felix and Marlene scrutinized from in front of it.

Such a scene and prospect invariably brought home to Michael how little ambition he had for anything more in life than he already possessed. The truth was, he could not for the life of him imagine how anything in this world could possibly be better than what he already had: to be preparing food for those he loved, with the prospect of sharing it with them. Perhaps if his own mother and father could still have been with them? But that was an old wound, and as near to healing as it was likely to be, in this age at least.

He was laying out plates and glasses on the big pine kitchen table when Figaro got up, shook vigorously and started fussing.

A dog's senses are, of course, far sharper than those of a man, but after a few minutes even the merely human ears of Michael could hear the front door opening.

"It's me!" came Cecilia's voice.

Figaro was already trotting off to greet her.

"It's finally over," she said some minutes later when she was properly in the kitchen and they'd exchanged a kiss. "We've charged Craig alias Saunders with conspiracy to murder Jack Hooper, as well as all his other murders, and now it's up to the Crown Prosecution Service."

"Is that likely to be a problem?"

"Probably not. Glyn Davies seems pretty confident we've given CPR enough to put him away forever. And of course, however it goes, there'll still be the Swiss at the gates itching to have a go at him."

"I think perhaps it may be some help to Adriana to know that you've got him," Michael said.

He returned to his table setting.

"I hope so," she said. "Verity's gone round to tell her. And I've been to see Leoma Walker." She paused. "There are some things you can't put right, however hard you try. But still, I suppose at least it's something good that we got it sorted before Jack Hooper's funeral. Ten o'clock tomorrow, isn't it? In the church?"

"It is. You'll be there?"

"I certainly intend to be. Have you been to see Adriana again?"

"This afternoon. She'll be all right. She's tougher than she looks."

As were most women, in his experience.

"Would you like a glass of wine?" he said. "This is nice."

"I would, actually."

He poured it for her and she took it, but for the moment did not drink from it.

"Adriana may be tough," she said, turning the wine glass in her hands, "but still I don't envy you having to preach tomorrow after all that's happened."

Again he nodded. No doubt they'd both been involved in enough appalling and seemingly meaningless griefs and disasters to be past attempting to explain or make sense of them—especially if 'explaining them' meant 'showing how they were good things really'. One could only trust there was meaning and reconciliation somewhere, and then do one's best to get on with life as it came: each joy, each sorrow, each pain, each pleasure, trying as far as one could to be an instrument of grace, always aware that with the best intentions in the world one could never be really sure how *anything* one did would turn out.

Montaigne, of course, made much the same point...

As for preaching... he would do what he always did at such times. He would get up very early in the morning and commend Jack Hooper and Adriana Martínez into the hands of God. He would read through the proper. And then he would wait. And listen. Something would probably come. It generally seemed to.

"Preaching is one thing," he said. "*You* had to solve the case."

"Just about everyone I know contributed to that. You included! Finding Gladstone Walker's body turned out to be crucial."

"Still, you pulled it off."

"Yes we did, thank God. Craig's as ruthless a killer as I've ever seen. And then he justifies it all with self-righteous twaddle and a load of racist crap." She twirled her glass gently, watching the wine as it swirled. "You should have heard him this afternoon, ranting on about what a patriot he is. Or on second thoughts you shouldn't. It would have made you sick."

Michael shook his head. "I dare say that patriotism and treason, like beauty, are very much in the eye of the beholder."

"In the end though, I found him rather pathetic. I suppose these egomaniacs always are. Once they're locked up."

He nodded. "Right." And then after a pause, "Once they're locked up." He paused again. "Though I suppose," he said finally, "none of us knows what we might have been like—given the wrong influence at the wrong moment. When I think of what I once was, it's something of a miracle I'm not just as evil as Craig is. Assuming of course that I'm not—which I dare say isn't mine to judge anyway."

She raised an eyebrow. Of course she knew what he was talking about.

"Well," she said, lightening her tone, "as our friend Jane would put it, you'll just have to subdue your mind to your fortune. You must learn to brook being happier than you deserve."

He chuckled. "Yes," he said, "I dare say I must."

There was a pause while he made a couple of adjustments to the table.

Rachel appeared in the kitchen doorway.

She was carrying a large Pyrex dish with pieces of chicken on it. Rosina was behind her.

"Ciao mama!"

"Ciao tesori!" Cecilia said, laid her still un-tasted glass of wine on the table, and bent to be kissed. Then, turning to Michael, "So what's for supper? Something chicken-y, I take it."

"Ah! You observed the pieces of chicken and then drew upon your fiendishly clever powers of detection and deduction?"

"Exactly. No flies on me!"

"Well it's British classics tonight—as specially requested by your mama. Chicken casserole with potato cobbler, and then apple crumble with Devon cream."

"Yum," said the detective superintendent. She picked up her wine, again swirled it around the glass and finally took a sip. "Indeed, very possibly double yum."

Sixty-Seven

Heavitree Police Station, the Chief Superintendent's office.
At about the same time.

"My thanks and my congratulations to you and your team," Sir Bernard said. "This is excellent news. You have solved your murder—and a number of other murders too, I understand. And the chances of a conviction are good."

Glyn Davies nodded. Sir Bernard had called him on his secure line just as he was about to go home. He glanced at the clock on the wall opposite him, decided that Olwen would not miss him if he were twenty minutes later than he'd said he would be, and sat himself back down behind his desk.

"I talked to CPR this afternoon," he said, "and they seem pretty confident we've given them more than enough. And I gather the Home Office are giving the Swiss permission to come over and interview Craig as well. So I dare say even if something does go wrong with our case, they'll be lining up behind us to pounce on him."

"Excellent."

"I presume all this means that your little problem at Thames House is sorted out, too? The monster is now dead?"

Sir Bernard chuckled. "I think it is. Decapitation is generally fatal."

"What about Ashley-Cooper?"

"To be fair to the man, there's no evidence he was anything worse than slow to see what was going on under his nose. But slow to see won't really hack it here, so he's taking early retirement."

"And, if you don't mind me asking, sir, what about that whole section?"

"Of course I don't mind you asking. It's been broken up. It's hard to be sure which of them if any were actually on board with Saunders'—or I suppose I should say, Craig's—weird and treasonous ideas. But it's come to light there have been several other foul-ups that originated in that section. Worst of all, they ignored a whole *series* of advance indicators to a bombing until it was too late. People *died*. It'll be bloody embarrassing, but if you ask me, at some point later this year that's going to come out and then we'll have to come clean and apologize publicly about it."

He paused for moment.

"Anyway," he said, "regardless of whatever happens over that particular screw-up, the section has been dissolved. Everyone in it's been transferred to a position where they'll have no access to anything sensitive. And we'll have our eyes on them. I dare say many of them will get the message and look for a career change. We'll encourage them in that."

"That's tough."

"I dare say it is," Sir Bernard said. "But Caesar's wife must be above suspicion."

EPILOGUE

Outside St Leonard's Church of England School, Exeter.
The following Monday afternoon, 8th October.

Cecilia, with Figaro beside her, had already been sitting in the car outside the school for several minutes when she heard the closing bell ring. She looked up. After a few minutes children began to emerge from the big glass-panelled double doors. At first they came out in twos and threes, and then in much larger groups. And now—she had not seen her approach—here was Rachel, already standing by the car, satchel in hand, and beside her, also satchel in hand, a beaming Tabitha Timms, who despite being frizzy haired and freckled and wearing glasses was actually rather pretty when she smiled.

"Tabitha wants to say to hello to Figaro," Rachel said.

"Oh! Yes, yes, of course," said a somewhat surprised Cecilia.

Appropriate doggy introductions were made. Figaro performed graciously, naturally assuming—as was, to be sure, his habit—that it was only right and proper for him to be the centre of adoring attention. So there was much waving of tail and patting of head.

"Can Tabitha come home to tea with me tomorrow after school?"

"Yes, of course you can, Tabitha. We'd love to have you."

"Thank you, Ms Cavaliere," Tabitha said, "only please can you telephone so mummy knows when to come and collect me afterwards? Here's the number. Mummy would come across now only she can't leave the car because of making a traffic jam." As she said this, she pointed across to a silver-grey Audi in the midst of a mass of cars, with a dark-haired woman in it who smiled and waved. Cecilia waved back.

"Will you tell your mama I'll call her this evening around six if that will work for her?"

"Thank you, Ms Cavaliere. I'm sure it will."

Tabitha darted off to her mother. Rachel meanwhile scrambled into the front seat beside Cecilia, and Figaro withdrew to the back.

"Tabitha's nice and she makes me laugh," Rachel announced— in Italian, which she and Cecilia always spoke when they were alone together.

Cecilia gazed at her for a moment, then on sudden impulse reached across, seized her daughter and hugged her.

"Mama, are you all right?" Rachel said, her voice somewhat muffled by her mother's hair. "You've gone all weepy (*piagnucolosa*)!"

Cecilia nodded and let her go just as Figaro, not to be excluded from a family hug, wriggled between the seats and insisted on his share in it.

She sat back. She wasn't sure she could speak.

"I do love you," she said when finally she could get something out.

Her daughter looked at her curiously while absent-mindedly scratching Figaro's ear. Then, after a moment's further thought—

"And I love you too," she added matter-of-factly.

Cecilia laughed.

"Of course you do!" she said. "Put Figaro where he's safe and put your seat belt on. We're going home."

THE AUTHOR'S
ACKNOWLEDGEMENTS
AND THANKS

As always, some things in this story are true or based on truth (so far as I know what the truth is), some things are made up, and some I borrowed from other people.

To begin with, I know nothing whatever of the inner workings of MI5—as will no doubt be obvious to anyone who does. My MI5 "sections", one of which might become a "rogue organization", are my own fantasy enriched by confused reminiscences of occasional James Bond movies and one or two searches on Google for answers to particular questions. The fact that one of those questions was, as I recall, "What is Thames House?" will give the reader some idea as to just how unbounded was, and indeed is, my ignorance of the subject.

If this story had been written by someone else, and I were shown it and asked which element in it I considered especially unlikely or implausible, I think I would probably say, "The contents of the report on United States Advanced Weapons vulnerabilities that Joseph Stirrup is alleged to have discovered." I would be wrong. The report of the U.S. Senate's General Accountability Office pointing to the vulnerability of the United States' advanced weapons systems to cyber attack was an actual report. The only thing I have made up is that I have MI5 being shown copies of it rather early (that is, some time before 12ᵗʰ September 2018) and the version Joseph sees reveals details of the systems examined and the methods by which their capabilities could be undermined. The report was in fact only published in October of that year, and for security reasons no particular weapons systems were cited. Nonetheless, according to one reporter,

> GAO investigators examined the findings of Pentagon cyber security assessments over a five-year period, from 2012 to 2017. The testers were tasked with trying to find vulnerabilities, in part by hacking into the weapons systems.
>
> In some cases, they were able to gain complete control of systems using simple techniques. The report describes one instance in which testers guessed an administrator password in nine seconds. In other cases, they shut down a system simply by scanning it—a typical first step in trying to carry out a digital attack.
>
> The testers managed in some systems to manipulate what the soldiers operating the weapon were seeing on their computer screens. In another case described in the report, weapons testers "caused a pop-up message to appear on users' terminals instructing them to insert two quarters to continue operating."[1]

The truth is, I wouldn't have dared make such a thing up. The amazing thing is, I didn't have to.

I borrowed the notion of a murderer killing someone on a boat

1 Elias Groll, "Many US Systems are Vulnerable to Cyberattack" in *FP* October 19, 2018; cf. an earlier paper by Stephen D. Bryen, "Dealing with Vulnerabilities of U.S. Weapons Systems" in *DefenseNews* March 29, 2017. Both of these pieces are available online.

out at sea and then hiding on the boat until it was towed back into harbour from an episode of the BBC's *Death in Paradise*—a series which is, incidentally, great fun, and has the virtue of never taking itself too seriously.

As always, I must thank my group of wonderful friends and colleagues who are kind enough to read this stuff through, point out my obvious errors, and again and again prevent me from making an even bigger fool of myself than I do anyway: first of course Wendy, who continues to put up with me, and then Renni Browne, Suzanne Dunstan, Chris Egan, Julia Gatta, Kara Kosaka (who designs wonderful covers for me), Jill Mather, Shannon Roberts, and everyone at The Editorial Department. Thank you all, very much, for continuing to look at my pieces of trivia, thereby encouraging and indulging me in the enormous delight I get from writing them!

Christopher Bryan,
The Annunciation of Our Lord to the Blessed Virgin Mary, 2019.

About the Author

Photograph by Wendy Bryan

Sometime Woodward Scholar of Wadham College, Oxford, Christopher Bryan is an Anglican priest, novelist, and academic, now semi-retired (whatever that means). He and his wife Wendy have lived for many years in Sewanee, Tennessee and Exeter, England, now planning to retire to Exeter. His earlier novels include *Siding Star* (Diamond Press, 2012), which was named to Kirkus Reviews Best Books of 2013, *Peacekeeper* (Diamond Press, 2013), *Singularity* (Diamond Press, 2014), *A Habit of Death* (Diamond Press, 2015), *The Dogleg Murders* (Diamond Press, 2016) and *Black Ops* (Diamond Press, 2017). Author and critic Parker Bauer in *The Weekly Standard* Book Review describes them as "ideal antidotes to the crypto-farces of Dan Brown." Bryan's numerous academic studies include *Listening to the Bible: The Art of Faithful Biblical Interpretation* (Oxford University Press, 2014), *The Resurrection of the Messiah* (Oxford University Press, 2011), the popular *And God Spoke* (Cowley, 2012) (which was among the books chosen as commended reading for the Bishops at the 2008 Lambeth Conference), and *Render to Caesar: Jesus, the Early Church, and the Roman Superpower* (Oxford University Press, 2005).

For more information about Christopher Bryan go to his website at www.christopherbryanonline.com or check his "Author Page" on Amazon.co.uk or Amazon.com

Lightning Source UK Ltd.
Milton Keynes UK
UKHW040631161219
355467UK00001B/323/P